Forty minutes later, I was clambering down a brick wall in pitch darkness, wearing wrap-around sunglasses and a black balaclava, with boot-polish smeared across my face and Barney's camera and Jenks' torch jammed into my back pockets.

It occurred to me that I should have sneaked Barney's camera out of his bag earlier in the day. Then I could have got one of the little kids to pose as a dead body with a bread-knife handle sticking out of it and taken a photo. Or made some warhead gadgets out of stuck-together kitchen equipment and run off a few pictures of them. Then Barney would have got a real shock when he got his film developed.

As it was, I was about to break into a room that probably contained nothing more than sixty bottles of spare loo-cleaner and a mop. Come tomorrow, we'd have to start all over again with a new Agent Z plan.

Also available by Mark Haddon:

Agent Z Meets the Masked Crusader
Agent Z and the Penguin from Mars
Agent Z and the Killer Bananas

For older readers:

The Curious Incident of the Dog in the Night-Time

GOES WILD

MARK HADDON

RED FOX

AGENT Z GOES WILD
A RED FOX BOOK 0099400731

First published in Great Britain by The Bodley Head Children's Books, 1994
First published by Red Fox, 1994

This Red Fox edition, 2003

3 5 7 9 10 8 6 4 2

Papers used by Random House Children's Books are natural, recyclable products made from wood grown in sustainable forests. The manufacturing processes conform to the environmental regulations of the country of origin.

Red Fox Books are published by Random House Children's Books,
61–63 Uxbridge Road, London W5 5SA,
a division of The Random House Group Ltd,
in Australia by Random House Australia (Pty) Ltd,
20 Alfred Street, Milsons Point, Sydney, NSW 2061, Australia,
in New Zealand by Random House New Zealand Ltd,
18 Poland Road, Glenfield, Auckland 10, New Zealand,
and in South Africa by Random House (Pty) Ltd,
Endulini, 5A Jubilee Road, Parktown 2193, South Africa

THE RANDOM HOUSE GROUP Limited Reg. No. 954009
www.**kidsatrandomhouse**.co.uk

A CIP catalogue record for this book is available from the British Library.

Printed and bound in Great Britain by
Cox & Wyman Ltd, Reading, Berkshire.

Psychokinesis

It was a Thursday evening when things began to go seriously wrong.

We'd just had our tea. Mum was practising her Turkish ready for our summer holiday, and watching *Wallaby Springs* on the telly. Dad was sitting at the dining table mending the sandwich-toaster which blew up at the weekend when I dug out a burnt waffle with the bread knife.

Me, I was practising my powers of psychokinesis. Sitting on the mantelpiece was a revolting porcelain sculpture of a shepherdess and a lamb which Mad Aunt Gwen had sent us for Christmas. I was trying to destroy it with my psychic powers.

On screen, Bruce Doggett, the Wallaby Springs vet,

was leaning over a hospital bed crying, 'Irene! It's me, Bruce. Come on, babe. Wake up.'

Irene had 46 tubes up her nose.

A doctor patted Bruce on the shoulder. 'She's in a coma, Mr Doggett. And I'll be straight with you, mate . . .' They went in for a close up. 'She may never recover.' Bruce's tears were drowned by the theme tune.

'Kaç kişi geliyor kokteylinize?' said Mum.

I focussed hard. Energy was flowing out of my eye-sockets. 'Set mind-lasers to maximum,' I said to myself. 'Take aim . . .'

'The main item tonight,' announced the newsreader, 'is the arrest of millionaire businessman Don Grundy on fraud charges.'

I shut my eyes and squeezed my brain-muscles. 'Fire!'

There was a sudden crash. Mum screamed and Dad yelled, 'Jeezamarooni!' I opened my eyes. The shepherdess was lying in several pieces in front of the gas fire.

I leapt to my feet, cheering, 'Yo! I'm psychokinetic!'

Except I wasn't, of course. I looked again. The shepherdess had been decapitated by the soldering iron Dad had hurled across the room. He was livid. He looked as if his head was about to explode. Something was horribly wrong. You had to stand on one of his Elvis records to make him this cross.

'What's happening?' I asked.

'Put a sock in it, Petal,' Mum said. 'Just for a tick.'

'Grundycorp plc ceased trading this afternoon,' continued the newsreader, 'along with its 47 subsidiary companies: the Nibbly-Biscuits chain, the Donburger fast food outlets, Funshine Tours . . .'

'Mum . . . ?' I whispered. I was worried. My parents seemed to have gone totally bananas.

Mum gave me a tired look and picked the holiday brochure off the coffee table. I could see the photos of the Moralim Bozuldu hotel, where we were going to stay, the games room, the gym, the Olympic pool, the long, white beach. Mum flipped the brochure shut and showed me the cover. In big, yellow letters across the top were the words, 'Funshine Tours'.

'Guess who won't be going on holiday this year?' she said.

'Ah . . .' I slumped onto the sofa.

'Excuse me,' said Dad, standing and heading for the door. 'I'm just going down the garden to shoot myself. I won't be long.'

'Mr and Mrs Sidebottom,' said the smiling newsreader, 'have decided to christen the quintuplets Jackie,

Jilly, Justin, Julian and Janice.'

Actually, it was Mad Aunt Gwen who had psychic powers. She must have sensed something terrible had happened to her Christmas present. She rang thirty seconds later. Mum put down her liqueur chocolates and stomped out into the hall.

I picked up the shepherdess, took out my chewing gum and used it to reattach the two heads, the lamb's head on the shepherdess, the shepherdess's head on the lamb. A big improvement.

And then it started to sink in. No games room, no gym, no Olympic pool, no long, white beach.

I nicked three liqueur chocolates and went into the kitchen. Badger, our stone-deaf, geriatric mutt woke up and clambered out of his basket, yawning dog-breath at me. I stuffed a chocolate in my mouth. It tasted of lavatory cleaner. I took it out of my mouth and threw it to Badger. He failed to see it coming, and it stuck to the top of his head.

Mum and Dad reappeared at opposite doors.

'That was Gwen,' explained Mum.

'Just what we need . . .' said Dad, who is not a Mad Aunt Gwen fan.

'Actually, it might be,' continued Mum, mysteriously. 'I told her about the holiday and she said . . .'

A look of horror began to spread across Dad's face.

'. . . and she said, well, they're going up to Blakeney to stay in a caravan that fortnight and, since we're not going to get a holiday, would we like to join them?'

Dad looked at me. 'Tell me I'm dreaming, Ben. Tell me this is just some hideous nightmare.'

'Sorry, Dad,' I said. 'This is really happening.'

He put his head in his hands and staggered back out into the garden.

Mum and I looked at each other. I said, quietly, 'You're actually going to go, aren't you.'

'Now, Ben, don't you start . . .' she said, wearily. 'Gwen is a warm, kind, loving, generous person. She is also my sister.'

So, she was going to go. And we would be going with her. I felt sick.

'Come on, Ben,' said Mum. 'Look on the bright side. It's better than no holiday at all.'

Mum was wrong. Being eaten by piranhas was better than sharing a caravan the size of a space capsule with Mad Aunt Gwen, four Siamese cats, a screaming baby, Uncle Roger the man-mountain and 37 porcelain shepherdesses.

I was about to say this when I noticed the time. Six-fifty. Ten minutes till the Crane Grove Crew meeting.

'Got to move,' I said, grabbing Badger's lead.

As I was clipping the choke-chain on, Mum bent down, picked the gluey chocolate out of Badger's head-fur and sniffed it. 'Mmm . . . Crème de menthe. Badger? Have you been at my . . . ?'

'Come on, Kiddo! Walkies!' I hit the accelerator and aimed for the front door before the investigation started.

Warp Factor Five

I've always found it hard to believe that Mad Aunt Gwen and Mum are sisters. There are no similarities. Mum's got a brain for a start, even though she switches it off for *Wallaby Springs*.

Mad Aunt Gwen, on the other hand, hasn't got a brain at all. She calls me 'Poochums' and wears cardigans with bobbles on. Her hobbies are knitting woolly things to go over her spare toilet rolls, using lots of air-freshener and collecting the pukey nick-nacks they advertise in Sunday magazines: plates with pictures of scotty-dogs on, little crying clown-dolls, porcelain shepherdesses, that sort of thing. Dad and I call them 'gwennies'. We get one every Christmas.

Uncle Roger has a problem with his glands, according

to Mum. I reckon he's got a problem with chocolate biscuits. If he was Japanese, he could be a Sumo wrestler, except he isn't Japanese. He used to do Morris Dancing. Then his back went twang. Now he lies on the sofa a lot and makes ships-in-bottles.

He also thinks he's the world's No. 1 child entertainer. Whenever we pay them a visit, he grins and says, 'What do you say to a game of hide-and-seek, young nipper?' Which is OK, except I'm not five years old and he'd need an aircraft hangar to hide in.

As for Baby Felicity, she just screams and poohs.

The lead jerked in my hand and jolted me out of my daydream. I'd missed the park gates, and Badger didn't want to do any extra walking. We turned back.

I cut round the boating lake to avoid the weirdo conducting an invisible orchestra outside the old café, ducked into the undergrowth and squeezed through the hole in the fence, dragging Badger after me.

According to Agent Z rules, I was meant to keep strictly undercover from now on. But I couldn't be bothered. When your summer holiday has just been gwennied, you can't put your heart into commando-crawling through a hundred metres of mud and nettles and crisp-packets. I walked straight past the rusty bulldozer and round the back of the old park-keeper's cottage. I let Badger off his lead and untangled the knotted rope from behind the drainpipe.

'Catch you later, Doggo.'

I hauled myself up to the first floor window and slid the mouldy plank aside. Once inside, I rolled the rope up and made my way downstairs.

Barney and Jenks were sitting in the Command Centre waiting for me.

'All crew now present and correct, Captain,' said Jenks.

'Ignite boosters,' replied Barney.

The room had been totally revamped. They had done some serious work the night before, while I was at the football with Dad. We'd started the redecoration last week. We'd made a huge oval screen on the main wall, painted the inside black and covered it with thousands of dots to make stars. Barney and Jenks had now covered the other walls with baking foil and lined up the three armchairs facing the space-window.

'Fasten your gravity-belts,' said Barney, in his best James T. Kirk voice, 'I'm charging the laser-drive.'

'Barney,' I complained, 'I'm not in the mood.'

'Fasten your gravity-belt, Ben, or those g-forces are gonna turn you into custard.'

'OK, OK,' I grumbled, sitting down, picking up the ends of the dressing gown cord attached to the arms of the chair and tying them across my lap. Jenks stuck an old bike helmet on my head then went back to his own chair, picked up his own helmet, sat down and strapped himself in.

'Neutrino shields in place,' continued Barney, leaning forward and twiddling the dials on an old gramophone we had found in the skip behind the Citizen's Advice Bureau. 'Hyperspace co-ordinates fixed. Let's get this bucket off the ground, lieutenant.'

'Yes indeedy,' said Jenks. 'En-gage.'

There was a sudden, shrieking roar from somewhere. Then Barney and Jenks tilted their armchairs backwards for two seconds, sucking in their cheeks on account of the g-forces. When their chairs were back on four legs, Jenks leant over and said, 'Barney put a pencil in his mum's food-processor and recorded it with his Walkman mike. Good noise, isn't it.'

Barney removed his helmet. 'Cruising in hyperspace. 943 zph. She's lookin' good, boys. Stand easy.' He cut the accent and turned to me. 'Hi, Ben. How's it going?'

'Don't ask.'

Barney, Jenks and I were the Crane Grove Crew. Our headquarters was the old park-keeper's cottage. The council had boarded it up years ago, but we'd broken in two summers back and turned the lounge into our Command Centre. We hung out here most evenings, cruising in hyperspace, cooking up plans and scanning the park for enemy insurgents with Barney's binoculars.

The three of us had been friends since First Form. I'm not exactly sure why. We didn't have a lot in common. But the Crew was a fixture now, like Sainsbury's, or the FA Cup Final, or tomato ketchup. You couldn't imagine life without it.

Barney was fat. It was the first thing you noticed about him. But he was too sussed-out to give a monkey's about that. And, besides, if anyone teased him about it, they'd soon find themselves head-down in a waste-bin.

Mum thought he was 'charming'. He was like that with grown-ups. He'd say things like, 'That's a very chic silk blouse, Mrs Phelps,' or 'How's the new Escort, Mr Lanchester? I hear the ABS braking system works like a dream.' And they'd lap it up.

Jenks, on the other hand, was as sussed as a face flannel. He never said the right thing, to anyone, ever. His family were barking mad, all of them. The last time I went round, his little sister Brenda broke her ankle playing duvet-cover parachutes from her bedroom window, and I had to do a truly world-class goalkeeping dive to stop baby Wayne pushing a box of matches into the bar-fire.

Jenks was skinny and hyperactive, with hair like a loo-brush. Somehow, his homework was always eaten, or burnt, or stolen before he got it out of the front door. Mr

Dawson called him 'the brain-drain'. And Mr Dawson was right. Jenks was not a bright boy.

Barney cooked up the idea of Agent Z last summer. The term was long and hot and tedious and life needed spicing up a bit. So, we started playing practical jokes under the code name Agent Z.

We put plastic tarantulas in the school gravy. We put clingfilm over the loo seats. And when Mr Forsyth, our history teacher, punished us by making us dig his garden we wired kippers to the underside of his car engine.

The summer term got spiced up good and proper.

For weeks on end, people kept finding hardened papier maché in their football boots, or worms under their duvet. And, whenever they did, there was usually a note reading 'with Love From Agent Z' lurking somewhere nearby.

But who was Agent Z?

Nobody knew. Except for us. We wore Z badges under our lapels, and kept diagrams and photos of Agent Z's successful missions on a notice board in the Command Centre. We swore a vow of secrecy and promised to obey the Agent Z Code of Honour until death.

We were swift and cunning and invincible.

Well, almost invincible.

Even Agent Z couldn't help me now. In a fortnight's time, I'd be trapped on a caravan site in Blakeney, and Barney and Jenks would be hundreds of miles away. Agent Z would cease to exist.

Barney walked over to the broken but impressive-looking fridge, poured Fanta into three Esso mugs, jammed a lemon slice onto each rim and threw in a couple of wrinkly glacé cherries. He handed one of the drinks to me.

'OK. Get it off your chest, Ben,' he said, in an uncley sort of way.

I got it off my chest. Don Grundy. Funshine Tours. The scuba-diving lessons. Mad Aunt Gwen. The Siamese cats and the woolly bog-roll-thingies. Everything.

They were sympathetic, but not sympathetic enough. They'd never met Mad Aunt Gwen. They didn't understand.

I pressed the point. 'And you two'll be going somewhere brilliant, I suppose?'

'Dunno,' replied Jenks, 'Like usual, I guess. Dad'll just wait for the work to slack off, then say, "Everyone into the van" and we'll get ten minutes to pack and find the tents.'

It sounded fine to me. Last year they'd gone to Scotland, and had a brilliant time, even though they'd had to turn back 150 miles up the M6 when his mum realized they'd left Wayne playing in the back garden.

'And you?' I asked Barney. 'Acapulco? Monte Carlo? Bermuda?'

'Nah. Nothing like that.'

'So?' I asked. He was hiding something. I could tell. 'Like what?'

Jenks was doing a head-stand against the space-screen. He said, 'Barney's got the last place on that Outward Bound Trip to Wales from school.'

'I hate you,' I said quietly to Barney.

'Aw, come on,' he answered soothingly, patting me on the back. 'It's nothing special. Look . . .' He took the Plas Y Cyfoglyn poster from inside his baseball jacket and unfolded it. 'Abseiling. Climbing. It'll be terrifying, Ben. You know me. I haven't got a head for heights. All those mountains they'll make us walk up . . . I'll need oxygen. And look at this. White water canoeing. Imagine being upside down in that stuff. It's not a question of fun, Ben. It's a question of coming back alive . . . more like joining the army than going on holiday. Nah. Give me two weeks in Blakeney any day.'

I wasn't sure whether he was winding me up, or trying to be nice. Either way, I wanted a grand piano to fall on his head. I said, 'I'm going home.'

He slipped back into Kirk-speak. 'You can't go through the airlock while we're in hyperspace, Buddy. You'll be vaporized in the quark stream. Half a nano-second, then, "Whammo!". There'll be bits of you from here to Ursa Minor.'

'Good,' I said, heading upstairs.

When I got home, Mum was standing in the kitchen next to the sandwich-toaster with the soldering-iron in one hand and a huge smile on her face.

'You mended it,' I said.

'Sometimes, these things need a woman's touch,' she explained. 'Fancy testing it?'

'Okey-dokey.'

I switched it on, took out the bread, butter, sugar and bananas, and stuck a mug of milk in the microwave for some hot chocolate.

'He stole a Brandy Barrel and a Grand Marnier, too, you know,' said Mum, crouching next to Badger and shaking her head at him. 'Naughty dog. I don't know what's got into him these days.'

'Senile dementia?' I suggested. 'Where's Dad, by the way?'

'Still outside.' She stood up. 'Major sulk, I'm afraid.'

I did a second banana-toastie and put another mug of milk in the microwave.

I found Dad at the bottom of the garden, sitting on a Gro-Bag in the dusk. He was playing my pocket Battlestar game and listening to Elvis Presley singing *Heartbreak Hotel* on the battery cassette player.

I sat down next to him. 'Have a hot chocolate.'

'Cheers, Ben.'

'Peeong! Peeong! Peeong! Bip! Peeong!' went the Battlestar game.

'Major sulk, Mum said.'

'Perceptive woman, your mother. What's your highest score on this thing?'

'84,600.'

'Bip! Bip! Peeong! WAAAAAH!'

'Oh, mallards,' said Dad. '22,350.'

'Now since my baby left me, I've found a new place to dwell,' crooned Elvis, 'down at the end of Lonely Street, at . . . Heartbreak Hotel.'

'Don't dodge the asteroids,' I explained. 'Aim straight for them, then press the FIRE button just as you make contact.'

'The problem is,' explained Dad, 'she's too nice, your mum. She just can't say no. Now, if Gwen was *my* sister . . .'

'Peeong! Peeong! Bip . . . !'

'Imagine the enemy cruisers are little caravans . . .' I suggested.

'WAAAAAH!'

Dad dropped the game and picked up the hot chocolate. '300. I'm too old for these things, Ben.'

'Tell you what . . .' I bit into my toastie. 'Mum can go to Blakeney, and you and I can go youth hostelling in the Lake District. What do you reckon?'

'Don't tempt me,' Dad tutted.

'I made you a banana toastie, by the way,' I said, handing it over. 'No sugar in yours.'

'Cheers, mate.'

'I'm so lonely . . .' wailed Elvis. 'I'm so lonely . . . I'm so lonely . . . I could die.'

'Besides,' I said, 'you're not allowed to be depressed. You're the grown-up. I'm the one who's meant to be depressed.'

He got stuck into the toastie. 'I'm sorry to have to tell you this, Ben, but being a grown-up isn't . . . Arghkhch!'

There was a dull cracking sound from inside Dad's mouth. He spat the contents onto the palm of his hand. In amongst the chewed banana and chewed bread was a shiny lump of tooth and a large knobble of solder.

'What on earth . . . ?' he asked, nursing his mouth.

'A woman's touch,' I said.

Big-Snack!

It started as low throbbing in the air behind the shower block on the far side of the caravan site. Within seconds you could see a massive cube of orange light shimmering a metre above the ground. The grass began to smoke and blacken. The cube hardened and the outlines of two cyberlizards took shape inside. There was a brief, screaming sound like big air-brakes, then the cube vanished and the five-ton raptoids dropped onto the burnt soil. Hot slime ran out of their steaming nostrils and the sun flashed on the stainless steel of their long, ridged muzzles.

A small boy, dressed only in a towel, came out of the shower block, looked at them, looked away, rubbed his eyes, looked again, wet himself and fainted.

The cyberlizards ignored him. The bigger of the two glanced at the bio-sensor welded onto its arm and pointed towards a small, pink caravan with net curtains parked at the far end of the site. They were at the door in five strides, effortlessly vaulting a Ford Fiesta and crushing a small tent under their gruesome, horned claws.

The shorter cyberlizard bent down to sniff the roof of the caravan, its acid nose-slime stripping the paintwork horribly. It knocked on the door.

A small voice from inside said, 'I'll get it, Roger love.'

Aunt Gwen didn't even see it coming. Her head was halfway down its throat by the time she got the door open. The raptoid lunged again at bullet-speed and wolfed the rest of her. Two pink slippers sitting on the 'Welcome' mat were the only remains.

The cyberlizard burped loudly and ran a carbon-fibre slash-claw over its lips to clear away the shreds of mauve nightie while its partner crouched to squint through the window. Uncle Roger was manoeuvring himself away from the breakfast table.

'Big-snack! Big-snack!' grunted the raptoid.

Its muscled foreleg tore through the flimsy wall and whipped him straight out of the jagged hole into its drooling jaws. It stopped chewing only to atomize an escaping Siamese cat with its deadly nipple-lasers.

'Next?' it growled, casually halving the empty caravan with its thrashing tail.

Cyberlizard No. 1 punched four buttons next to the screen built into its third knee and scrutinized the luminous readout.

'Grundy, Don Grundy. Pentonville. 47 degrees south-west. 234 kilometres.'

Cyberlizard No. 2 grinned a three-metre, stainless steel grin, picked a lump of fat from between its razor-teeth and said . . .

'Come on, move it, Ben. You're already ten minutes late for . . . Honestly, look at you. Sometimes, I think you might actually be clinically insane.'

I came to abruptly. My pyjama-top was round my neck and I still had only one leg inside my boxer-shorts.

'OK, Mum. I'm moving.'

Mum's wrong. I'm not clinically insane. But there might be a screw loose somewhere. Most people dream at night. I seem to do most of my dreaming during the day. Mum and Dad give me a hard time about it, but they haven't got a leg to stand on, I reckon. It's like liqueur chocolates or Elvis Presley. It's something to do when your brain's switched off, except that it's not fattening and it doesn't sound like an elephant seal on heat.

I'd been doing a lot of it since Don Grundy got banged up and our summer holiday in Turkey went down the tubes.

I threw my clothes on, skipped doing my teeth, ran downstairs, grabbed a chicken-leg from the fridge and hit the road.

I wanted to see Barney and Jenks. I hadn't been to the headquarters over the weekend. I couldn't summon the energy, and I didn't want to hear Barney saying how much he was going to hate Plas Y Cyfoglyn. I'd caught the major sulk virus off Dad. I played myself at Scrabble.

I watched snooker on the telly. I increased my Battlestar score to 90,550. I took Badger to the adventure playground, sat on the swings and had death-fantasies about Aunt Gwen and Uncle Roger for two hours, then came home again, completely forgetting I'd had Badger with me, and had to spend another two hours looking for him.

But today, I was going to pull myself together. If I avoided Barney and Jenks for the next week and a half, I'd really regret it when they disappeared off on their holidays.

I walked up to Barney in the playground and turned my lapel so he could see my Z badge.

'Greetings, Earthworm,' I announced.

'With knobs on,' he replied.

We gave each other five.

And it was then that we saw the bruise coming towards us. It was huge and purple and it was smack in the middle of Jenks' forehead.

'What happened?' I asked.

'Duvet-cover parachutes?' suggested Barney.

'Nah,' replied Jenks. 'Much better than that.'

'Well . . . ?' I said.

'It was yesterday evening, like,' explained Jenks. 'I'd just gone round to Bazzer Griffith's house. 'Cos he said I could borrow his geography homework. Except he's got this glandular fever thing going round and his mum wouldn't let me in because it's really infectious, you know, like cholera or rabies. So, I was coming back down the hill and there was this ice-cream van. And I was just scoffing a ninety-nine when I saw Potato-Head cycling down the hill at about sixty miles an hour. And, suddenly, I noticed this flea-ridden dog bumbling across the road. Mangey old thing, bit like your dog, Ben, come to think of it. So, anyway, I shouted, 'Look out, Sir!' But he just turned round and said, 'Yes. Lovely evening, Jenkinson.' Deaf berk. And then it was too late. He saw the dog and hit the brakes, and it was like it was all happening in slow motion. He missed the dog by about two millimetres but slammed into the ice-cream van and somersaulted straight through the back window. The dog didn't seem to notice anything at all. It just wandered off towards the adventure playground.'

'Yep. Senile dementia,' I said, feeling rather relieved that no-one had stopped to read Badger's name-tag.

'What are you on about?' asked Jenks.

'Go on,' urged Barney. 'Don't take any notice of him.'

'Oh yeh. Right. So, there was glass everywhere and Potato-Head's legs were sticking out of this back window and all you could hear was the ice-cream van dinger playing *Oranges and Lemons* over and over again. It was totally mega. Anyway, then the ambulance came, and the best thing was, someone found the top of Potato-Head's ear on the pavement. It must have come off when he went through the window, like. And this ambulancewoman, she put it between two choc-ices and they took it to the hospital with them so they could sew it back on . . .'

And then Barney said, 'Mmm. . Catch you later, boys. Got to see a man about a horse.'

He turned and disappeared into the main building. This struck me as weird, but I was too interested in the gory details to wonder what he was up to.

'So,' I said to Jenks, pointing at his forehead, 'you haven't explained how you got this bruise.'

'Oh, that,' he replied. 'I was laughing so much, I turned round and walked into a lamp post and knocked myself out.'

In assembly, Sunil, who lives down the road from us, gave a short talk about Hinduism: how Shiva has four arms and three eyes, and chopped his son's head off then stuck an elephant's head on instead. All that business.

It sounded a bit odd to me. I mean, Sunil decided to become a Baptist last term, because if you go to the Baptist chapel on Sundays you qualify for judo lessons at their Youth Centre, and their preacher happens to be a black belt who was in the last Olympics.

Still, he seemed to know his stuff.

After the talk, Breezeblock stood up and said she had some rather unfortunate news. Mr Dawson had been involved in a road-accident over the weekend. She would be sending him a get-well-soon card and anyone who wished to sign it should pop into her office today.

For some reason she didn't mention the fact that Potato-Head had dived through an ice-cream van, but then she's never had much of a sense of humour.

'Mr Dawson will be returning to school sometime next week. Until then, his classes will be taken by Mrs Chimnoy. And I think that's just about . . .'

Mr Lanchester leaned forward and whispered something at her bottom. 'Oh, yes. I almost forgot,' she continued. 'As a result of the glandular fever which seems to be laying everyone low at the moment, there are now two free places on the Outward Bound Course at Plas Y Cyfoglyn at the end of term. If anyone thinks they might like to go, they can get forms to take home from the school sec . . .'

I grabbed Jenks' collar and hissed, 'Run!'

We had a painful collision with a dinner trolley at the corner of the entrance hall. Three plates got atomized and the back half of Form 2D's egg-box dragon came off the wall. But we arrived there before anyone else, which was the important thing.

I stood panting at the door. 'Mrs Goldstein . . . The forms . . . for the Outward Bound thing . . . Breezeblock . . . sorry, I mean Mrs Block . . . she said . . .'

'They've all gone, I'm afraid, Ben.'

'Gone?'

'All thirty of them. It was most peculiar. 3B trooped in before assembly. They seemed very keen.'

'Oh . . .' A huge weight descended on me. I wanted to lie face-down on the floor and not get up, ever. Why was everything going wrong? Perhaps it was Gwen-Voodoo. Perhaps there had been an evil spell on me ever since I decided to psychokinetically smash the porcelain shepherdess. I reminded myself to swap the heads back after school in case it neutralized the magic.

A phone rang.

'Sorry, Ben. There's not a lot I can do.' Mrs Goldstein picked up the receiver. 'Oh, hello Mrs Collins . . . So, little Jimmy's no better then . . . ? Yes, I know. They're going down like flies here . . .'

Jenks and I trudged off towards English.

Five minutes later, we were reading this poem by a bloke called Ted Hughes. Mr Hughes is a bit over-sensitive and writes about crows and foxes and sheep as if they're all crazed psycho-killers. It's kinky, but it's better than getting all lovey about daffodils.

At the end of the class, we had to write our own poem about animals. I was stumped until I remembered the cyberlizards. They'd really have appealed to Mr Hughes, I reckoned. I uncapped my biro and, for the next half hour, I didn't think about Plas Y Cyfoglyn once.

My best lines were:

Their snot
was hot.
They grabbed the fat man
From inside the caravan,
And gnashed and slurped
And gobbled and burped.

Mrs Carmichael said it was 'interesting, but rather disturbing'.

Barney was nowhere to be found during break, so I sat on the cycle racks while Jenks moaned about his big sister, Julie, who works on the till in the Co-op. She'd just joined this heavy metal band called *Thrashfist* and bought herself a drumkit. Jenks was looking for a tent he could borrow so he could sleep in the garden.

After break, we did the Crusades with Mr Forsyth, which were loads of yobs on horseback going to the Holy Land to kill people and burn towns, rather like Chelsea fans, except that this was Christianity not The European Cup so they thought it was alright, apparently.

We caught up with Barney at lunch. I clunked my plate of styrofoam quiche onto the table and sat down. Jenks squeezed in opposite.

'Those forms,' I said, glumly. 'They'd all gone.'

'I know,' said Barney.

'3B came in and nicked them before assembly,' explained Jenks.

'Crafty, eh?' agreed Barney.

'Barney,' I said, 'what's up with you today? I need some sympathy here.'

'Wrong, kiddo,' replied Barney. 'What you need are application forms.' He filled his face with a forkful of quiche, then reached into his pocket and took out a sheaf of xeroxed papers. He handed one application form to me and one to Jenks. 'I'll burn the rest tonight,' he added, slipping the remainder back into his pocket.

'But how did you know . . . ?' I asked.

'Elementary, my dear Ben. Like Jenks said, Bazzer's got glandular fever. And I saw him snogging Karen Bottomley outside the chippie on Friday night, so she must have it, too. They were both booked in for the trip. And you can't abseil with a temperature of 140.'

I leapt to my feet and yowled like a Ted Hughes psycho-killer moose, 'Yeeee-harrgh!'

The room fell silent and Mr Lanchester glared at me from the staff table.

'Before you get too carried away,' Barney had his calculator out now, 'I'd like to point out that bribing 3B was a costly job.' I sat down again as he tapped the keys. 'You owe me for twenty-nine Mars Bars and one six-pack of sugar-free Ribena for Trish Manilow who's diabetic. Let's call it a round fiver each . . .'

'And Barney's already going, and Jenks is going to offer to do some work helping his Dad painting and tiling this big house out in Boddington in September to help pay so that he can go and . . .'

Mum and Dad sat there gawping as I drivelled. It was not Good Tactics. Good Tactics was to come in, cook your own tea, do all the washing up, make Mum and Dad a coffee, hoover the lounge, maybe, or clean the cooker, let them get their feet up and then introduce the subject casually. But I was too desperate for Good Tactics.

'. . . and Barney said that you were sensible people so you'd probably have holiday insurance, which means you'll get most of your money back, and the trip only costs £150 which is about the same as a plane ticket to Istanbul, so it wouldn't really cost you anything in effect . . .'

Dad lifted one eyebrow. 'Has your friend Barney ever thought of going into politics?'

I was on the right track. Dad was softening.

I ploughed on. 'And like Barney says, it'll be character-building, because there'll be canoeing and orienteering and rock-climbing and stuff and it will make me more mature and improve my professional management skills which is why all these businessmen go on this sort of thing . . .'

Mum turned to Dad. She had a warm and kindly smile on her face. I could almost see the thought-bubble over her head, reading, 'Oh go on, why not let him go?'

Dad tried to look stern but couldn't keep it up. He always was a sucker for Mum's warm and kindly smiles.

'If it's too expensive, I could always take my bike and my Walkman and the radio-cassette to a car-boot sale and see what they'd fetch . . .'

'Ben?' asked Dad.

'What?'

'If I say yes, will you shut up?'

'Scout's honour.'

'Give me the form,' he said wearily. I gave it to him. 'A fortnight of you going on like this and I'd probably end up strangling you. I suppose £150 isn't much to pay if it keeps me out of prison.'

'You are a seriously mega guy, Dad.' I gave him a hug: just a medium-sized one, enough to show how grateful I was, but not so much as to make him embarrassed, because he's not a New Man and can't handle soppiness. Then I gave Mum an extra-big hug and a slurpy kiss because she can handle it by the bucketful. 'Thanks. You're both mega.'

I rounded up Badger, grabbed five quid of pocket-money from my plastic Batman-bank to pay Barney's bribery costs and headed off to the park before they changed their minds.

You could tell, from a hundred metres away, that Jenks' Dad had said yes, too. I could see him trying to do cart-wheels on the far side of the boating lake as I came into the park. Even hyperactive people don't do cartwheels unless they're pretty cheerful. When I reached him, Jenks was lying in the contents of a knocked-over waste-bin.

'So, your Dad let you go?' I said, looking down at him.

'Oh, hi, Ben.' He took the chip-paper off his face. 'Yeh. I'm going to help him with the big house. He said it was about time I learnt how to do some decorating so I could join his business some time, 'cos no-one was ever going to employ me doing anything else.'

'You could be an acrobat.'

'Very funny, I don't think so . . . And you?'

I gave him the OK sign.

'Jackpot!'

Badger in tow, we headed off towards the hole in the fence. I was back in the mood now, so, when we'd squeezed through, we did the undercover stuff, with knobs on. We broke off loads of leafy branches, stuck them in Badger's collar and through our trouser belts, gripped a couple in our teeth, then crawled and shim-mied from tree-trunk to shrub to bulldozer round to the back of the headquarters and scrambled up the rope.

Barney could tell from the sound of our laughter that Plas Y Cyfoglyn was on. When we appeared at the foot of the stairs he threw us our cycle helmets and said, 'Strap 'em on, boys. The Higgs-Boson Propellors are ready to roll.'

We tied ourselves into the armchairs.

'Ignition,' he announced. 'Cut support-gantries. Yes indeedy, we have go-go-go.' He twiddled the dials and hit the button on his Walkman. We heard his mum's food-processor trashing the pencil, pushed our chairs backwards and sucked in our cheeks. The high-pitched whine slowed down and a trumpet fanfare started. Barney had been adding to the tape. The music reached a climax, then gave way to Barney's microphoned voice saying, 'Agent Z. Stardate 3009 AD. Summer holidays, the final frontier. Your mission: to seek out new civilizations, to abseil down cliff-faces, to canoe through white-water rapids, to climb vast mountains, to boldly have a wild and crazy time where no kids have had a wild and crazy time before.'

The tape clicked off.

Barney turned to us. 'Welcome aboard, boys.'

'Yo!' said Jenks.

'Yo!' I agreed. 'We're with you all the way, Captain.'

We were in hyperspace.

Countdown

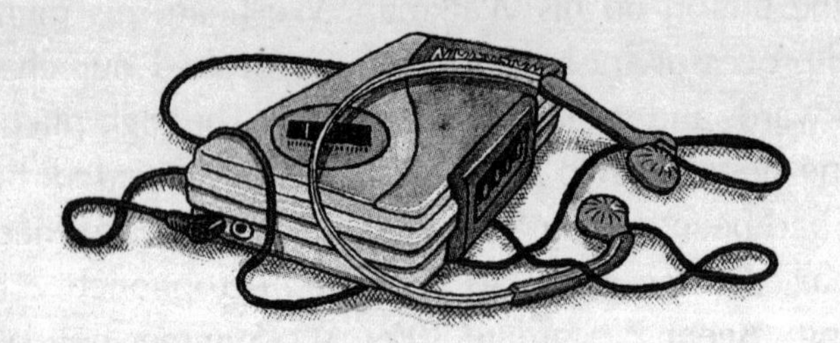

The last two weeks of term flew past.

We got the forms in and Mr Lanchester OK'd them. 'So . . .' he said, recapping his biro, 'all three of you are coming, then? I do hope you're not planning to gang up and create havoc.'

'We shall be far too busy improving our professional management skills,' said Barney, who knew just how far to push it. 'By the way, Sir, how's your eskimo-rolling?'

'Watch it, young man,' replied Mr Lanchester darkly before retreating into the staffroom.

Potato-Head Dawson returned to school, his right ear in bandages just as Jenks had predicted. The story had done the rounds by then and he couldn't walk down a corridor without someone whistling *Oranges and*

Lemons. He pretended that the bandages had made him temporarily deaf.

Every evening, after school, we honed our canoeing skills by paddling an oil-drum round the boating lake with Barney's cricket bat. We practised abseiling from Jenks' bedroom window, laying his mattress on the patio to avoid a repeat of the parachuting disaster. And we made a trial ascent of the back wall of the gym-block joined together by five knotted skipping ropes, and did it rather well, despite the fact that Archie, the caretaker, had to get us down with a ladder.

At home, Dad was still having trouble getting used to the idea of two weeks spent cooped up in a caravan with a ten-ton morris-dancer and a cat-fancier in a lilac cardigan. Mum didn't help. She kept teasing him by saying things like, 'Roger and you can have hours of jolly fun playing hide-and-seek.'

I took pity on him. I emptied the last of the cash out of the Batman-bank and bought him Battlestar II to help pass the time while he was sitting sulking in the dark outside the caravan.

'And, here, you can borrow my Walkman, too. Then you can listen to lots of Elvis without driving everybody up the wall.'

'What do you mean . . . driving everybody up the wall?'

'I mean . . . they probably won't have your exquisite taste in music.'

Dad gave me a wry look, then smiled. 'Cheers, Buster.'

'Hang on in there, Dad. You'll pull through.'

We did the Magna Carta. We did pie-charts. We made a rainfall-metre. And we beat the Woodside C-team fifty-seven-nil at football thanks to Jenks. He poked their captain in the eye and started a riot. He got sent off together with seven Woodsiders, including their goalkeeper. After that it was a walkover.

To celebrate the beginning of the summer holidays, Barney splashed out on fourteen packets of multi-coloured pansy seeds. We climbed over the school gates one evening and sprinkled them in a giant Z on the lawn outside the main doors. Hopefully, they'd be coming up by the time we got back from Wales.

Back in *Wallaby Springs*, Irene had begun to flutter her eyelids, even though the doctors had said her brain was dead. So you knew she was going to recover just in time to find out that Bruce Doggett had fallen in love with Shirley who worked in the coffee-bar.

A judge sentenced Don Grundy to ten years in prison. He also had to call in the police when Grundy was pelted with rotten fruit by loads of would-be holiday-makers. They looked as if they'd all been forced to spend a fortnight locked in a caravan with their mad aunts.

Then, suddenly, it was all over. It was the last day of term and we found ourselves sitting in assembly listening to Breezeblock saying goodbye to Mrs Phelps who was going off to have a Phelplet, and to Mr Twombley who was going to teach English in Indonesia. Why they needed to speak English there I wasn't sure, unless Koala

TV Inc. wanted to beam *Wallaby Springs* into Jakarta without sub-titles.

'It only remains,' concluded Breezeblock, 'for me to wish you all a very happy and productive summer holiday . . .'

Stampede.

Mum thought a suitcase would be the most sensible thing, but I stood my ground. This was a rugged, manly, outdoor kind of holiday, not a wimpy, beach-paddle kind of holiday. So, I went next door and borrowed a rucksack from Mr Zsinewski who walked from Land's End to John O'Groats last year raising money for some kidney-scanning gizmo. Mum said it made me look very rugged and manly and outdoor. I told her she was just jealous.

I packed my penknife, my compass, my torch, six

pairs of chunky socks, a luminous cagoule, Battlestar I, three jumpers, four T-shirts, a tracksuit, grippy gym shoes for cliff-scaling, nine bars of chocolate in case I got buried in an avalanche, and fourteen pairs of clean boxer shorts to keep Mum happy.

I took out the Doc Martens I'd got for Christmas, polished them with Grubber's Patented Waterproof Dubbin to repel bog-water, then laced them on.

I went downstairs and watched the last seven shoot-outs in *The Sicilian Connection* with Dad, did my teeth, lay down on the bed and closed my eyes . . .

. . . Barnioso, Jenketti and I were screaming down the autostrada in the Ferrari. Fifty metres ahead was the Cadillac containing the godfather Don 'Concrete Over-coat' Grundini and his huge, stubbled henchmen.

Without warning, revolvers appeared from the Cadil-lac's passenger windows on the end of pin-striped arms. Bullets started to prang and whizz off the Ferrari's red paintwork. We ducked below the dashboard and Barney zig-zagged the car crazily across the busy lanes.

The speedo quivered into the red and I could smell burning rubber. An exit slipped past and the Cadillac lurched to the right, over the hard shoulder and up the steep, grass slope towards the roundabout. Barney heaved on the wheel. A concrete bridge-support loomed sickeningly then disappeared, tearing a rear-side panel off the car.

With an ear-popping bang, we ripped through the crash-barrier onto the slip-road. Barney took the round-about at seventy, slewing the car round the cab of a braking juggernaut. Then the Cadillac appeared again. But the sunroof was open now, and a suited Italian powerlifter was rising out of the hole, a three-metre bazooka in his hands. Barney pressed his foot to the floor.

And then the Cadillac vanished.

Instead, coming towards us, was an ice-cream van, driven by a shepherdess in a morris-dancing costume. A large crème de menthe liqueur chocolate sped out of a side road and rammed the ice-cream van. There was runny green goo and runny brown goo everywhere. Elvis Presley stepped out of an ambulance and started singing, 'Oranges and Lemons . . . doo-wop, doo-wop . . . sang the bells of St Clements . . . woppy-doo-bop . . .', which wasn't part of the plot at all.

It occurred to me that I was falling asleep, and that I should make an effort to take my Doc Martens off and get under the duvet. But it was too late. My legs wouldn't move and my brain had already gone fuzzy.

Fog and Lipstick

I got Mum and Dad to drop me off early just in case the Gwen-voodoo was still working. I wanted time to sprint for it if we ran out of petrol or found the road blocked by a fallen tree.

Consequently, I was the first to arrive. Dad hoiked my rucksack out of the boot and we said our farewells.

'Be good,' insisted Mum. 'And be careful. I don't want you coming home on a stretcher.'

'They don't call me "The Mountain Goat" for nothing,' I said.

'I thought they called you "The Boy Who Trod On His Own Shoelace And Fell Over While He Was Carrying The Class Fish-Tank",' Mum replied.

'That was two years ago, Mum . . .' I complained.

'Look after yourself, kiddo,' said Dad, butting in to head off an argument.

'You, too, Dad.' I shook his hand, then turned to Mum. 'And you be nice to him. I think he's very brave going with you.'

'I promise,' said Mum. 'Scouts' honour.'

Out of the corner of my eye, I saw Mr Lanchester herding a gaggle of children through the school gates. On the far side of the street, Barney was climbing out of his Dad's Granada.

Mum had seen them, too. 'Now, give your mumsy a big, smoochy kiss, Ben,' she grinned.

'Not just now, Mum,' I said, stepping backwards out of range. 'Have one on credit. And enjoy yourselves in Blakeney.'

Mum was not going to be outdone. 'Bye-bye, then, Poochums!' she said, in an unnecessarily loud voice.

'Bye-bye, Grandma!' I shouted back.

Mum and I grinned at each other. Dad looked down at his shoes and shook his head. I missed them already.

And then I didn't miss them at all, because a rusty, white van, with 'R. Jenkinson – Painter and Decorator' written on the side, was rattling to a halt outside the gates. Jenks leapt out, dragging his luggage after him, and the van sped away. No goodbyes, no smoochy kisses, nothing.

I strolled over to Barney and we watched Jenks wrestle his bags to the bench.

'Kevin was playing tiggy-off-ground with some friends,' Jenks explained, still panting, 'and his mate

Chris was going round the bathroom off-ground so's he could get out the bathroom window and down onto the kitchen roof and he slipped and kicked the sink off the wall and there was this huge waterspout and it was coming down the stairs and Mum's got everyone running round with buckets and Dad's rushing to pick up some plumbing gear from uncle Kenny . . .'

'Hi,' said Barney flatly.

'Oh right, yeh,' said Jenks. 'Hi.'

We gave each other five and flashed our Z-badges.

Then Jenks said, 'God . . . there're girls going!'

I turned round. Jackie Phipps and Mel Carver were sitting on two huge rucksacks reading *Cosmo* and shrieking like jackals.

'Sort of,' said Barney. 'Except, on the girls' course they do wild flower arranging and paint watercolours.'

'Oh . . .' For a second or two, Jenks fell for it.

Barney chuckled and slapped him on the back. 'What century are you living in, eh?'

'Your sister's a girl and she plays in *Thrashfist*,' I added.

'All you have to do,' continued Barney, 'is show your natural male superiority when you're climbing those cliff-faces.'

Jenks gave Barney a sarcastic smile. Mel Carver threw the discus and javelin for the county schools' team. She could have beaten Jenks up Ben Nevis carrying a fridge any time.

Girls weren't the only surprise. Despite his bandaged ear, Potato-Head was still joining the expedition.

'And before we go any further,' he announced loudly, 'I would like to point out that I am *off duty*, and anyone who is tempted to whistle *Oranges and Lemons* will get a thick ear. Understood?'

Mr Lanchester, who was only off-duty when he was unconscious, gave Potato-Head an uneasy look. He seemed worried that his colleague might be more trouble than the kids.

'Right,' he said. 'Is everyone here?'

'I'm not,' said Jenks, who thought it was hilarious.

'Lord preserve us,' said Mr Dawson wearily, 'a comedian.'

Mr Lanchester did the roll-call:

Winston Gregory. A quiet, arty kid who was planning to become a concert pianist. Winston's dad was a driver for Securicor. He was probably sending Winston to Plas Y Cyfoglyn to turn him into a real man.

The Incredible Hulk. A tiny Indian kid whose parents ran the Pleasant Price Grocery. Two years back he could hardly speak any English. On his first day at school, Barney saw him in the library, reading slowly from a comic, 'I . . . am . . . the . . . Incredible . . . Hulk . . .' Since his real name was Khalilbhala Khrishnakatalaranjitali, or thereabouts, it stuck. His English was now so good he could empty the boys' showers in two seconds with his Breezeblock impression.

Penny Threadgold. She had long, blonde hair and pink nail-varnish. She was obviously under the impression that Plas Y Cyfoglyn was a disco-and-shopping complex.

Babs Clifford. Penny's henchwoman. Babs was the school smoking and shoplifting champion and only went out with boys who had motorbikes and sideburns and criminal records.

Then Mel, Jackie, us three, and a gaggle of kids from the year below who I didn't recognize because they never did much except collect conkers and play sheep in nativity plays.

'Now,' said Potato-Head, 'when you've all got your bags and been to the toilet, and when Penny has finished applying her lip-gloss, I think we can climb aboard . . .'

We squeezed ourselves into the minibus, Barney, Jenks and me bagging the back three seats. Mr Lanchester took the wheel and the engine coughed into life. I looked out of the window as we pulled away and saw a small, blue sports bag sitting on the pavement. I asked around, but no-one claimed it.

'Serve them right, whoever it is,' said Potato-Head, gleefully. 'Hit the gas, Bob.'

Mr Lanchester threw his colleague a brief glance of outraged fury. I doubt even Mrs Lanchester was allowed to call him 'Bob'.

'Yo, Bob,' added Jenks. 'Got for it.'

Mr Lanchester hit the brakes so hard the tyres screamed. I headbutted Babs, Winston's Tizer hit just about everyone, and Jenks got the sort of shouting-at that you get when you let off a grenade inside an airliner.

We hadn't even reached the end of the street.

Within minutes Jenks was hyper again, demonstrating paddle-manoeuvres and inventing gory climbing accidents.

'. . . and when you reached the end of the rope it would go tight and cut you into two pieces, like a cheese-slice . . .'

'Oh do shut up, little boys,' said Penny Threadgold, flicking her hair out of her face and giving us her film-star glare.

'Calm down, Jenks. You're disturbing the ladies,' said Barney. 'Incidentally . . .' He leaned towards Penny, whispering confidentially, 'I'd blow your nose if I were you. You've got a bit of a dangley bogey there.'

'What? Oh, I . . . oh hell . . .' She fumbled desperately for a tissue, and carried on fumbling even when Barney started laughing, just in case she really did have a dangley bogey.

'Very funny,' she hissed, when her nostrils had been checked for cleanliness. 'You're so juvenile.'

Ten minutes later, Jenks slipped onto the floor, tied the laces of her suede boots to the seat-leg and stole the make-up bag from her holdall.

'Very fetching indeed,' said Barney, when Jenks had finished applying the vivid pink lipstick.

'What are you lot . . . ? Hey! Give that . . .' shouted Penny, swivelling in her seat. 'Gnkh!' she added, when the knotted laces stopped her swivelling any more.

Potato-Head was soon clambering down the aisle to do some refereeing. 'OK, OK,' he growled, wearily. 'Who wants to be dumped at the nearest train-station?' He noticed Jenks' make-up. 'Jenkinson, have you got some sort of personal problem?'

'Dresses. High-heels,' said Barney. 'Can't keep him out of them. Been seeing a psychiatrist for months.'

'Oi!' complained Jenks, thumping him.

The fight began again.

It was the usual sort of school trip.

Potato-Head caught The Incredible Hulk coughing on a cigarette in the gents' at the service station, but couldn't do much about it because he was having a secret cigarette himself, out of sight of Mr Lanchester.

Two small boys had a fight in the minibus, during which a pair of spectacles got hurled out of a window. So Mr Lanchester had to lead a search party back down the motorway. A police car stopped and the officer had a man-to-man chat with Mr Lanchester about road safety, but was very apologetic when he discovered the glasses by treading on them.

To cap it all, Babs was spectacularly travel-sick.

'You are *not* going to throw up, Barbara. Just pull yourself together,' insisted Mr Lanchester.

'But I *am* going to throw up, Sir,' insisted Babs.

And she was right.

In the horrified silence following the eruption, Barney looked at the spattered floor and said, 'You had the scampi and chips, then.'

It took forty minutes at the next Little Chef and eight buckets of borrowed hot water before anyone would set foot back inside the minibus.

We drove the next hundred miles with the windows open.

You could tell when we reached Wales because the rain started. The fog took a little longer to thicken up, but it was only a mile or two before we were driving through aerial custard. Like Barney said, you could run an Outward Bound Course in the centre of Scunthorpe in this weather and no-one would know the difference. Except Scunthorpe didn't have roads the shape and size of a cow's intestines.

We lurched and swerved and twisted. I stared at the window. Rain was the wrong word. Salmon could have swum up it. It occurred to me that being rugged and manly and outdoors might involve frostbite and death from exposure.

The holiday spirit had evaporated. The minibus began to feel like detention on wheels. I took out my Battlestar, but got zanged by asteroids every time Mr Lanchester hit a Z-bend. Barney started singing *Three Million Green Bottles* quietly to himself, accompanied by Winston on his portable electric mini-keyboard. And The Incredible Hulk tried to cheer us up by reading out the problem page from Mel's *Cosmo* in his Breezeblock voice.

We were passing through some fog called Llangrogwyn when Jenks remembered that it was *his* small, blue sports bag sitting outside the school gates. I said he could borrow ten pairs of my boxer shorts and Penny said she'd lend him a floral mini-skirt.

Night fell. I gave up playing Battlestar and began to regret lending the Walkman to Dad.

Winston, too, said he was feeling travel-sick. Mr Lanchester, whose patience was wearing thin by now, told him to stick his head out of the window until he felt better. Winston decided he wasn't quite so travel-sick after all.

We had been driving for so long that we should have been in Wyoming by now.

I slept.

Barney and Winston were down to 3,987,465 green bottles by the time we reached Plas Y Cyfoglyn.

A wooden sign flashed in the headlamps and the minibus swung through a stone gate onto a road made entirely of boulders. I was jolted awake and realized I had been snoring on Jenks' shoulder, where I'd dribbled horribly. There was a searing pain in my neck.

Mr Lanchester heaved on the handbrake and parked the minibus on what turned out, next morning, to be a flowerbed.

We were stretching our aching legs and gathering our bags when the passenger door opened and a head appeared. I hadn't seen a head like it since I came downstairs one night and found Dad watching *Suicide Platoon* on the sly. The hero was a psycho Vietnam corporal who could only say, 'Let's kick ass!' and 'Eat lead, sucker!' In the last scene, he blew his own head off with a grenade rather than get captured by the enemy.

The head had eyes like ping-pong balls and a three millimetre haircut. You could have moored an oil-tanker to its neck.

'Great stuff,' grinned the head, rubbing its hands. 'More victims!'

Rubber Sausages and Eskimo Rolls

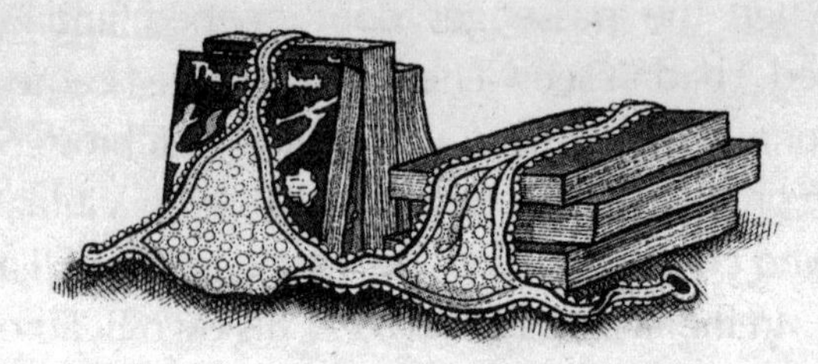

Grenade-Head waited for us to dump our rain-sodden luggage, ordered us into the main hall then clapped his big, beefsteak hands together to get our attention.

'Welcome to Plas Y Cyfoglyn. My name is Ed Michaels. I'm the Centre manager, and I shall be in charge of you lot for the next two weeks . . .'

The central heating was on the Siberia setting, but Grenade-Head was wearing a T-shirt. His bicep-veins were like power cables and his chest was so big he looked as if he was wearing a bra full of phone directories.

'It was lights-out half an hour ago, so I won't waste time telling you all about the Centre. But I shall just say this . . . I run a tight ship here. This is not a holiday camp.

This is a wilderness adventure training centre. You're not here to put your feet up. You're here to learn something. And learning it will depend on teamwork, hard graft and discipline. Now, I suspect that some of you are not terribly used to discipline.' It was Babs Clifford he was looking at, but he sounded as if he meant everyone, including Mr Lanchester. 'So, let's get one thing straight, right from the word go. I need 100% concentration, 100% of the time. So, when I say jump, you jump. Understood?'

He was terrifying. Some of the little kids nodded so hard they would probably have eaten their own legs if he'd told them to. For the first time in my life, I began to think that playing hide-and-seek with Uncle Roger might not be such a bad idea.

'Lights-out is at ten sharp. Breakfast is at seven sharp. No smoking. No drinking. No boys in the girls' dormitory. No girls in the boys' dormitory. And you will not, I repeat not, turn the place into a pig-sty.'

Mr Lanchester was staring at Grenade-Head the way teenage girls look at rock-stars. It was pure adoration. This man was leagues ahead of him in the child-control stakes. Mr Dawson, on the other hand, looked nervous. He was probably wondering where the nearest pub was, how he might get there, and whether he would be put into detention if he got caught.

Barney leant towards me and whispered, 'I wonder if they have room service?'

Jenks decided that the joke was so good he had to share it with everyone. 'Excuse me,' he said eagerly. 'Is there room service?'

I put my head in my hands. Barney put his head in his hands, and said, wearily, 'Ant-Brain strikes again'.

Grenade-Head walked up to Jenks and stood in front of him, the muscles in his leathery face twitching dangerously. He didn't go ape. He spoke very slowly and very quietly. 'That . . . was the very last piece of lip that I am going to get from you.' The effect was electric.

I was wrong. The haircut was from *Suicide Platoon*, but the delivery was modelled on Cyril, the librarian from *Blood Frenzy*, which some twerp at Megavideo put in my *Raiders of the Lost Ark* box a few weeks ago. When Cyril said, 'I don't mean to be rude, but I'm afraid I don't like you very much,' it was only seconds before the power-saw came out of his sandwich-box.

What he actually did with the power-saw I'm not sure, because Mum came in, realized what I was watching, ejected the tape and went to strangle the manager of Megavideo.

'OK,' barked Grenade-Head. 'Ten minutes, and I want you all in bed.'

We were standing in front of the dormitory plan when Mr Lanchester came up behind us, rubbed his hands together and said, gleefully, 'I think we are going to have an excellent time, aren't we, boys?'

I waited for Barney to say something funny, but he couldn't think of anything. Glumly, we picked up our bags and headed for the stairs.

Behind me, I heard Potato-Head say, 'Hey. Look at this. We're shacked up together, Bob.'

The brochure hadn't got the atmosphere of the dormitories quite right. Maybe scratch 'n' sniff photos were too expensive. Maybe if people knew they'd be sleeping in a cloud of sock-stink and mildew they wouldn't pay to come.

We fumbled our way through the dark and found our beds. I thought about brushing my teeth, but only for a millisecond. I excavated my pyjamas from the bottom of my rucksack, put them on and discovered that the heat from the minibus gearbox had melted two chocolate bars into the crotch.

'Maybe this wasn't such a good idea,' I said, climbing into my tracksuit. 'At least Aunt Gwen isn't a psychopath.'

'You've only been here . . .' Barney consulted his diving watch, 'twenty-two minutes and thirty-four seconds.'

'Quite,' I replied.

'Remember,' Barney insisted, 'Agent Z is tough and invincible. He is not put off by mad skinheads and chocolatey pyjama-crotches. He also needs his beauty sleep. Sweet dreams, Benjy.'

I gritted my teeth and climbed under the stiff, damp sheets.

They weren't sweet. They were bizarre. When I woke up I was having this nightmare about being stuck inside a caravan full of Siamese cats. Knight Crusaders had set light to it and the fire-brigade were putting it out.

I sat up, rubbed my eyes and noticed the rain spattering against the window, which explained the fire-brigade bit. But an alarm bell was still going like the clappers, and Jenks was screaming, 'Fire! Fire! Run! Help! Fire!'

I leapt out of bed, grabbed my DMs, Battlestar and penknife, then realized that there was no fire.

An older boy with a towel draped over his arm and a floppy, cricket-captain hairstyle walked past Jenks, said, 'It's the breakfast bell, you damn prat,' and disappeared into the washroom.

The alarm stopped.

Jenks turned to me. 'Er . . . just testing, Ben.'

I shook my head, dug the Tesco's bag of bathroom-gear from my rucksack and headed for the washroom myself.

'Morning, gentlemen,' Barney said to the cricket captain and his giraffe-sized friend, taking out his Mickey Mouse toothbrush and Homme Sauvage anti-perspirant.

The cricket captain gave us the kind of look you give to a piece of dog-poo squashed onto the sole of your trainers. Then his mate accidentally turned his tap on too hard, spraying water everywhere.

'Flood! Flood! Help! Run! Flood!' he screamed.

They thought it was the joke of the century.

Jenks shook his flannel at them like a loaded rifle. 'You just wait, you scummy, snotty, pathetic, snotty . . .'

'Cool it,' said Barney, lowering Jenks' flannel-arm. 'I haven't got the energy to break up a fight this early in the morning.'

It seemed such a waste. Their parents obviously spent thousands of quid a year getting their sons educated at some posh boarding school. And they were still wazzocks. We could have knocked them into shape at our school for free. But perhaps that wasn't the point. Perhaps if you had kids like that, you were willing to spend thousands of quid a year to make sure they didn't come home every evening.

Still fuming, Jenks de-smelled his armpits and the cricket captain showed off by wet-shaving his totally hairless chin. Barney rolled on some Homme Sauvage and wandered to the far window.

'Odd . . .' he said casually, walking back to the sinks. 'You can see right into the girls' changing room.'

The two wazzocks were at the window in a nanosecond.

'The one on the far right . . .' explained Barney, taking the top off the cricket captain's toothpaste and squeezing the tube to suck the paste back in. 'Just above the heating vent.'

His timing was perfect. He had taken the top off his athlete's foot cream, squeezed a couple of centimetres of it into the toothpaste, replaced both caps and gathered up his stuff before either of them had turned round.

'Come on,' he said to us. 'Let's hit breakfast.'

We got to the foot of the stairs just in time to hear Potato-Head saying, 'It was like an aeroplane taking off, Bob.'

'Snoring is natural,' replied Mr Lanchester. 'Leaning out of the window to have a cigarette is something you should have grown out of fifteen years ago . . . Ah, good morning, boys.'

We turned into the dining hall.

The fried bread was like lino, and you could have built a road-block with the sausages. A week of this and surviving in the wild by eating hawthorn twigs and rabbit droppings was going to seem like staying at The Ritz.

While Barney ate our three breakfasts, Jenks drum-soloed on the cutlery and I used my penknife to carve a model aircraft carrier out of a particularly solid sausage. Then Grenade-Head gave us five minutes to get into warm, waterproof clothes and assemble in the hall.

Waterproofed and assembled, we were introduced to the other members of staff: Tanya, who was vacuum-packed into a pair of jodhpurs and looked like she'd just stepped out of the *Horse of the Year Show*; Brian, who had a pony-tail and a moustache so vast and bushy you could have swept roads with it; Lesley, the canoeing instructor, and a host of other outward bound types with beards and chunky jumpers and no flabby bits.

Grenade-Head then explained that we were being arranged into teams because 'learning to work together and take orders is an important part of wilderness adventure training'.

It had just clicked that we were in imminent danger of being split up, when Barney said, 'Yeh, yeh. Hang on, I'm thinking, Ben.'

Grenade-Head got started. Mel Carver went into the Red team with a freckled midget. Babs Clifford got put into the Blues together with a giant green cagoule which might or might not have contained a human being. And the Yellow team acquired a small girl wearing a Snoopy baseball cap and a spherical boy whose idea of warm, waterproof clothing was an Arsenal scarf.

'Excuse me, Sir.' It was Barney. A plan had formed in his brain.

'Yes . . . ?'

'I hope you don't mind me asking . . .' He inched forward and lowered his voice, as if he was about to do the dangley-bogey joke. 'But do you mind terribly if I could be in a different team from those two.' He turned and threw a glance at Jenks and I. 'Both of them are pains in the butt.'

Grenade-Head sucked in a deep, irritated breath. But it was Mr Lanchester who spoke first. He could read Barney like a book.

'Mr Michaels,' he said, 'I really don't think you should take any notice of . . .'

Grenade-Head interrupted him. 'Don't worry. I can handle this, Bob.' Mr Lanchester winced and shut up. 'Now, young man.' Grenade-Head turned to Barney. 'I don't think you heard what I said, did you. Teamwork is about getting on with people whether you like them or not. So, I am going to teach you a lesson. You will be in the Greens. And so will they. And I want to see the three of you getting on like clockwork. Is that clear?'

Mr Lanchester shook his head sadly as Barney turned to us and whispered, 'Agent Z: One. Grenade-Head: Nil.'

Then Grenade-Head scored the equalizer.

'You two.' He looked down at his list. 'Justin Marchmont and Gregory Fforbes-Wilkinson. Green team.'

The two wazzocks from the washroom.

And as if that wasn't bad enough, he then gave us Penny Threadgold. Agent Z: One. Grenade-Head: Two.

Greeny number seven was a small girl called Eleanor Beasley. She looked lost and frightened, like she'd got on the wrong bus coming back from Brownies and ended up here by accident.

Number eight was Roz Winters. She was wearing dungarees and army boots under a plastic mac. The hair was shaved off the sides of her head and there was a tiny, gold ring in the side of her nose. I got the feeling that she and Penny were not going to spend the evenings discussing eye-liner.

Grenade-Head explained the day's activities and assigned a schoolteacher to each team. We got Potato-Head, which was a nice surprise for us, but a nasty one for him. While we gathered round Lesley, he sidled up to Grenade-Head and muttered, 'I . . . er . . . I was under the impression that we were, you know, here in a sort of . . . advisory capacity.'

Grenade-Head gave him the sort of look you give to someone who has a chicken growing out of their head. 'You mean . . . sitting around all day on your backside?'

'Well . . .' That was precisely what Potato-Head had meant.

'Nonsense. We all muck in here. Besides . . .' He patted Potato-Head's belly the way you might someone's Jack Russell. 'It won't do you any harm to work a bit of that off.'

Potato-Head made a last, desperate effort. 'But my ear . . .' he said, tapping the lump of white bandage attached to the side of his head.

'It's only canoeing, for goodness' sake,' Grenade-Head answered with tired irritation, already turning and walking away, 'not judo, or rugby league.'

'Team spirit, man,' said Mr Lanchester, chuckling to himself, as he walked past Potato-Head on his way to the abseiling equipment lockers. 'Team-spirit.'

'Okey-dokey,' said Lesley. 'Everyone here? Right. Let's have you all round the back and down to the jetty.'

We trudged out into the rain.

The three Submosauruses moved through the cold depths of the deep lake, as slow as storm clouds. The weak rays of green sunlight filtering down through the murky water threw dappled patterns on their massive flanks. Shoals of fish swarmed round them like birds banking round office-blocks.

They were bored. They'd been here since the Cretaceous period. The first three million years were OK because their brains were the size of peanuts and when your brain's the size of a peanut, eating, sleeping, swimming and going to the lavatory are all rather thrilling. But they'd evolved since then, and the lake had begun to seem pretty dull.

Once upon a time, they'd hung out on the surface, sunbathing, birdwatching, having mud-baths, playing catch with the moose and bears which came to drink at the waterline. Even the humans were no bother at first.

They just screamed and ran, and that was fine.

Then things changed. Suddenly it was all wrist-watches and camcorders and ABS braking systems and it didn't take the Submosauruses long to figure out that they'd better keep their heads down or they'd end up in laboratories with syringes in their bottoms.

But they were lonely. The fish were being particularly tedious this morning and those ten canoes bobbing about up there looked really inviting. They'd come up for a chat. Nice and slowly so as not to put the humans off. Warm up with some conversation about the weather and see how it went from there.

But something had gone wrong. Obviously they'd come up a touch too fast. The people in the canoes all seemed to be gibbering or throwing up. One man, whose head looked strangely like a potato, had leapt right out of his canoe and was thrashing about like a crocodile's lunch. The first Submosaurus realized that

man couldn't swim and reached out with its tree-sized foreleg to gently pick him up. But the Submosaurus wasn't very good at doing anything gently and the man burst, which was a bit unfortunate . . .

. . . I'd got canoeing wrong, you see. There wasn't a rapid in sight. It was just: how to paddle forward; how to paddle backwards; how to turn left; how to turn right; how to get out of the boat if you fell out, etc. etc. Then a long paddle down the lake in convoy, with Captain Prat and Fforbes-Giraffe chatting Penny up and Jenks butting in with comments like, 'Justin has a pink silk pyjama-case,' and 'Gregory keeps talking to matron in his sleep.'

Yawnerama.

Roz summed it all up. Back at the jetty for lunch, she said to Lesley, 'When are we going to do some proper canoeing? This is dead boring.'

'Yeh,' I said, 'eskimo rolls and stuff.'

Only towards the end of the afternoon did I realize that I should have kept my stupid mouth shut.

It was raining again, the greasy lasagne was still growling in my stomach and I was zipped up to the neck in a baggy, rubber wetsuit. Lesley was explaining how to do a rescue when someone has capsized: making a platform with your canoes to empty their boat and helping them back in, blah, blah, blah.

Fforbes-Giraffe showed Penny how cool and muscular he was by doing it first. Then Captain Prat did it. Eleanor Beasley refused to do it at all, but had to do it anyway when Jenks performed some spectacular acrobatics on my canoe and knocked her for six. Potato-Head said he was dying to have a go but he didn't want to get his ear infected.

'Now . . .' said Lesley, 'Roz was complaining that we weren't doing anything interesting like eskimo rolls. Well, we don't normally do them on the first day, but as you're so keen, and you're going to get wet anyway . . .'

She demonstrated the paddle-wiggles you did when you were upside down, then turned over and popped up again. It looked simple. Then Roz did it, so it had to be simple.

'Ben,' said Roz, shaking the water out of her hair, 'you wanted a go as well, didn't you?'

'Er . . . Well . . . I mean . . .'

Fforbes-Giraffe started the chant, 'Roll . . . roll . . . roll . . .' and soon everyone had joined in.

'It's alright, Ben,' said Lesley. 'If you don't want to . . .'

'I'm doing it,' I insisted. I did not want to be an Eleanor Beasley, especially in front of Captain Prat and Fforbes-Giraffe.

I flipped over.

Everything went black and fourteen litres of water scooted up my nose. I tried to remember the paddle-wiggles but left and right and up and down didn't seem to have any meaning any longer. I wanged the paddle this way, then that way, then let go of it altogether. I shouted for help and my mouth filled up. I tried to undo my spraydeck, but couldn't. It became suddenly clear that I was going to die. My life flashed before my eyes: climbing Snowdon with Dad; balancing the frying pan over my bedroom door to trap Santa Claus, knocking him out and discovering it was Mum; making a bomb with my new chemistry set and igniting Gran's lounge; Presley, my pet African Toad who was, himself, now dead.

'Wheee-up!'

Daylight flashed around me and I was hauled out of the water by my armpits. I retched something blobby onto Lesley's spraydeck and lay there coughing while Barney and Jenks emptied my canoe and Captain Prat and Fforbes-Giraffe laughed their socks off.

'Anyone else fancy a go?' asked Lesley when I had climbed back into my boat.

Not a word. Not even from Fforbes-Giraffe and Captain Prat. I was furious. They loved having a good laugh at my expense, but they didn't want anyone laughing at them.

'You pansies,' I said. 'You realize, don't you, that Penny never fancies anyone unless they can do an eskimo roll.'

'OK then,' said Lesley. 'Let's head back . . .'

'Just a minute,' said Fforbes-Giraffe, 'I think Ben wants another go.'

There was nothing I could do. The paddle whacked me in the ribs and I was upside down again.

I didn't bother with the roll-wiggles this time. I heaved myself straight out of the cockpit, turned myself into a human torpedo, and aimed for Fforbes-Giraffe's canoe.

It was like dominoes. I hoiked Fforbes-Giraffe's paddle. He keeled over, grabbing Barney's hair and taking him with him. Jenks whooped, swung his paddle over his head and whacked Penny Threadgold under the chin, knocking her overboard. Potato-Head reached out a helping hand towards her, she grabbed it, tried to climb up it and the two of them toppled over on top of me.

When I came to the surface again, Lesley was shouting, 'Mr Dawson! Can't you control these children?' Potato-Head was clasping the side of his head and groaning, 'My ear! My ear!' Eleanor Beasley was crying and Roz was shoving Captain Prat into the water while everyone was looking the other way.

Lesley was not happy. Back at the jetty, she barked, 'Get those canoes onto their racks! Now! And wait here!' She turned and stormed up the path to the Centre.

As we were heaving the boats out of the water, Roz thumped me on the back and said, 'Sorry, mate. That was mean of me.'

'No sweat,' I replied, playing it cool. 'I'll do it right next time.'

'Bet you won't,' she laughed. 'Took me two years to learn to eskimo roll . . . Uh-oh. Get your flak-jacket on.'

I turned round to see Grenade-Head stomping down the path like a rhinoceros planning to ram a Land-Rover.

'What the hell do you lot think you were playing at?' he bellowed, jabbing his sinewy finger at Barney, Jenks and me. 'Do you realize, you brainless little idiots, that someone could have drowned?'

'He started it,' said Jenks, pointing to Fforbes-Giraffe.

Grenade-Head exploded. 'Shut your trap!'

I saw a tiny blob of madman-dribble at the corner of his mouth and retreated a little to give me a head start if he went into a strangling-spasm.

'You girls, hop it,' he growled. 'You, too.' He pointed at Roz. 'Scram. I am not running a sideshow.'

'Just because I'm a girl,' she said, 'you think I had nothing to do with it, don't you? That's so sexist.'

'You what . . .?!' Grenade-Head was speechless.

I was impressed. But not half as impressed as I was when she turned towards Captain Prat, said, 'Well, I've got something to do with it now,' and punched him hard in the side of the head.

'That's it!' Grenade-Head roared. 'All of you. Run round the lake. Then do a hundred press-ups.'

Jenks looked down at his rubber wet-suit bootees and said, 'We can't run in these.'

Jenks was wrong. When Grenade-Head roared and lunged towards him, Jenks ran fast enough to qualify for the Olympics.

Room Service

When Jenks and I got back to the Jetty, Roz and the wazzocks had finished their press-ups. When Barney got back, we'd finished ours. So we hung around in case someone had to call an ambulance. When Barney finished his press-ups it was pitch-dark, but he was still alive, so it wasn't as bad as it could have been. Jenks and I took a shoulder each and helped him to the dining room.

Potato-Head was waiting for us.

He didn't shout. That wasn't his style. He just explained that if one of us had drowned, he'd go to prison for being irresponsible and we'd get lynched by each other's parents. Plus, if we mucked about again, he'd change teams with Mr Lanchester, and Mr Lanchester would have us on the first train home if we so much as burped in public.

'Oh, and I almost forgot,' he said, dumping four trays of food on the table, 'these were left for you.'

I scraped the cold, white grease off my slice of processed beef and sniffed at it. It smelt like someone's slipper-insole.

Agent Z: One. Grenade-Head: Seventy-Six.

Five minutes later we collapsed onto three comfy chairs in the games room to eat my emergency avalanche chocolate.

Roz Winters was thrashing the Arsenal Scarf at darts, and Potato-Head was watching the late repeat of *Wallaby Springs* with a clutch of little girls. Irene had completed her miracle recovery and was poking around Bruce Doggett's office while he performed an appendicectomy on the Reverend O'Malley's pet koala. She found the love letters Shirley had written to Bruce hid-

den under the worming pills. She read them and her face went all wobbly. She fainted backwards onto the desk and then they cut to Brad Toomey surfing at Shark Point so that you couldn't tell whether or not she'd had a relapse and gone back into her coma.

I leant over to Potato-Head. 'Didn't know you were a fan.'

He gave me a tired look. 'Ben, after a day being in charge of you three, even Mother Theresa of Calcutta would want to switch her brain off.'

'That's what Mum says,' I replied. 'You should try liqueur chocolates and Elvis Presley records.'

Potato-Head gave me a puzzled look and Barney said, 'Yes! That's it! Love-letters!'

'What's it?' asked Jenks. 'Where?'

'Conference, lads,' said Barney.

We trooped out.

Barney did the composing. I did the handwriting and Jenks nicked the perfume.

Captain Prat's letter read, 'Dear Justin, Wait for me in the canoe shed at midnight. Don't let anyone see you coming. And don't tell Gregory. I love you. Penny. XXX.'

Fforbes-Giraffe's read, 'Dear Gregory, Wait for me in the canoe shed at five minutes past midnight . . .' etc, etc.

We sprayed them with perfume, enveloped them and put the letters under their pillows. Jenks did some screaming in the washroom to get Miss Jodhpurs out of the office, Barney filched the key, undid the shed door, left it off the latch then, slipped the key back.

I slept for an hour. I was in the middle of manoeuvring my Leopard Attack Helicopter down onto the bucking deck of the USS Wisconsin when I was woken by Jenks, whispering, 'Yo, Ben. C'mon. Move it, move it.'

We crept downstairs and found Barney waiting by the pig-bins carrying a tray. On the tray were two bowls, two spoons, a packet of All-Bran, a pint of milk and a note reading, 'Room service, courtesy of Agent Z'.

'Perfect,' I said. 'Let's round 'em up.'

They fell for it hook, line and sinker. First Captain Prat, then Fforbes-Giraffe. Right on the dot, they slipped out of the centre and into the darkened shed. We shut the door behind them, retired to bed and let them stew until The Moustache went out for his dawn jog and heard them shouting for help.

But that wasn't the best bit. The best bit was the story they told Grenade-Head. Fforbes-Giraffe had gone to the loo in the middle of the night, apparently, looked out of the window and seen this suspicious figure trying to break into the shed. He'd woken Captain Prat up and the two of them had gone down to tackle the burglar. But – what do you know? – when they crept through the door, it shut behind them.

Extraordinary.

Even more extraordinary, Grenade-Head fell for it. He congratulated them on their bravery but told them to come to him next time. It didn't enter his head to ask why they needed to put their best clothes on and wear so much after-shave before tackling an intruder.

We got the third degree from Fforbes-Giraffe and Captain Prat, of course. And if it weren't for Barney's quick thinking, Jenks would have blown it altogether.

We were doing orienteering with The Moustache. We had a ten minute briefing, then trudged our way through ten miles of cow-pats, bogs, nettles and trouser-shredding thornbushes, picked up our ten pink doodahs and finally found our way back to the Land Rover and the packed lunches.

'That was an extremely unfunny joke,' snarled Captain Prat, whalloping the green-egg sandwich out of my hand, 'and you are going to be extremely sorry for it.'

'Oh . . . er . . . what joke was that?' gabbled Jenks. 'We didn't play a joke on them, did we. I mean . . .'

'No point in denying it,' shrugged Barney. 'They've guessed.'

'Hey . . . wait . . . no . . .' Jenks began waggling his half-chewed Penguin at Barney.

'Sorry,' Barney continued, taking a bite of his apple and smiling at Captain Prat. 'I thought you'd see the funny side of it. But there you go . . .'

My heart sank. I did not want those two getting their own back while I was abseiling down a hundred-metre cliff-face. 'Barney . . .' I said, 'are you sure you . . . ?'

Barney took no notice of me. 'Anyway, it wasn't poisonous.'

'Poisonous?' Captain Prat was thrown for a second or two. 'Don't wind me up, you little toerag.'

'The athlete's foot cream . . .' said Barney, innocently.

Captain Prat and Fforbes-Giraffe looked at each other in confusion.

'You obviously haven't been cleaning your teeth regularly enough, have you,' tutted Barney.

Captain Prat and Fforbes-Giraffe carried on looking at each other in confusion.

'Hang on a minute . . .' Barney continued, sounding surprised. 'You weren't talking about the toothpaste, were you. You were talking about getting locked in the shed last night.' He began to chuckle. 'Which means . . . Wait . . . There wasn't a burglar at all. Am I on the right track? And someone else tricked you into . . .'

'Shut it, fatso,' hissed Fforbes-Giraffe, jabbing Barney's face with his finger. 'You know nothing, OK?'

They turned and stamped off back to their own green-egg sandwiches.

Roz Winters was one hell of a lot brighter.

She came up behind Barney while we were standing on top of a hill faffing about with compasses and maps and looking for big things in the distance like mountains and church spires and football stadiums.

'Now, I *did* see the funny side of it,' she remarked casually.

Jenks forced a laugh. 'Oh, the athlete's foot cream. Yeh, right.'

She patted him on the head and said, 'He's very cute, but he's not very good at this sort of stuff, is he?'

'How did you know?' asked Barney, running his finger across the map while Jenks huffed.

'Bruce Doggett's love-letters,' she said. 'I was playing darts, remember?'

'Right,' said Barney, calmly. 'Give us some warning if you're going to shop us, yeh? We'll need to take evasive action.'

'Chill out,' she said. 'You can bury those two in concrete and drop them in the lake for all I care.'

'Brilliant idea,' grinned Jenks.

'Shut up,' I said, whacking him.

'Just one piece of advice,' she continued. 'Don't try getting your own back on Michaels. He's dangerous.'

'Just an ordinary, run-of-the-mill, deranged, Sergeant Major killer-type, I thought,' shrugged Barney.

She shook her head darkly. 'Not ordinary. Weird. Dead weird. I'll tell you something really freaky.' She shielded her eyes from the sun and gazed into the distance so that she looked as if she was doing the map-stuff. 'Like, I was having a poke round when we arrived yesterday, and I was trying to get into that little room next to the airing cupboard. You know the one? Anyway, Michaels came down the corridor and saw me and he went absolutely berserk. He said I was never to try and go into that room again, under any circumstances. I asked what was inside and he . . . he went sort of purple and started shaking and . . . well, I really thought he was going to flip out in a major way. Scared the living daylights out of me . . . So, just you be careful, yeh?' She turned and began to walk away. 'Catch you later, lads. And keep up the good work.'

Wooflets

Out beyond the barbed wire I could hear the barking of the chained Rottweilers and the screaming of the wind as it swept down off the mountains. Searchlight beams rotated slowly in the starless sky and, every now and then, a machine-gun barrel glinted in the darkness.

It was now or never. We knew what Grenade-Head was up to. We had broken into the locked room and seen the grinding machines. But we couldn't mend a broken padlock. Come morning, he would know. If we weren't out of here in four hours, we would end up like all the other kids, sliced into chunks and packed inside little tins of Wooflets Premium Grade dog-food.

I lit a match to read my watch. 3.24 a.m. My turn was coming up again. Six minutes and I would be back

underground, digging in the camped, hot tunnel, listening to the guards' boots tramping incessantly back and forth above my head.

I began to sweat . . .

'What do you think, Ben?' asked Barney.

'Er . . . about what?'

'Roz. Reckon she was just winding us up?'

I rubbed my eyes to drag myself back into real life. 'Nah. Why should she? I mean, she apologized for making me do that eskimo roll. And she shoved the cricket captain into the lake, right. She's got to be on our side.'

Barney agreed. Roz'd got the wrong end of the stick.

The locked room didn't come into it. Chances were, Grenade-Head was simply in a stinking mood. He'd cut himself shaving, or got some kind of food-poisoning from the grease on his processed beef. That was all.

But Jenks wasn't having any of it. He'd already decided that Grenade-Head was an international arms dealer on the run from Interpol, who had undergone plastic surgery and kept a cache of rifles, surface-to-air missiles and nuclear warheads next to the girls' washrooms.

'That is just about the stupidest idea you've had this year,' said Barney, taking toast-slice number five from his pocket. 'But . . . It's brilliant. I love it.' He folded the slice and chewed it whole. 'Listen . . . Here's the low-down. We break into the room after dark with a torch and my camera. We take photographs of the warheads, get the film developed down in the village, tip off Interpol, and sell the story to the *Daily Mail* for, what, three grand?'

'Ooh, five, at least,' I said. 'Enough to get us to the Seychelles next summer at any rate.'

'Incidentally, Ben,' said Jenks, turning to me. 'Can I borrow another pair of your boxer shorts? This pair's beginning to niff something horrible.'

We spent the day pony-trekking in the drizzle with Miss Jodhpurs. Goldie, Snubkins and Biscuit were half-horse, half-sofa and had been trained not to do anything dangerous like breaking into a trot. So, the sight of a rabid farm dog exploding out of a barn door and heading straight for us, teeth bared, was quite refreshing.

I gripped the reins and crouched down like John Wayne in *Stage Coach*. The snarling animal aimed for Eleanor Beasley. She screamed and fell off Cuddles into the mud. The dog bit Cuddles in the leg and ran away. Cuddles didn't seem to notice. Eleanor began crying again.

During dinner, we quizzed Winston about the Yellow team's rock-climbing and realized that Roz's description of Grenade-Head's major freak-out wasn't an exaggeration.

Half-way up the first ascent, Winston got the serious willies and froze. Grenade-Head barked at him but Winston's brain had short-circuited. He gave Winston ten seconds to get to the top before he undid the rope. Ten seconds ticked by and Winston didn't move. So Grenade-Head unknotted the rope. .Winston plunged five metres before the safety line twanged tight.

Jenks was wrong. It didn't go through you like a cheese-wire. But Winston was walking a bit funny nevertheless.

'I was only kidding about the warheads,' said Jenks, nervously, after hearing the story. 'Let's just, like, I don't know, put some soap in the tea-urn, or something, yeh?'

'I understand if you can't take the pace, Jenks,' said Barney, holding out his hand. 'All you have to do is give up your Z badge and we'll say nothing more about it.'

'OK, OK, I give in,' said Jenks, eventually. 'But if your stupid plan goes wrong, and Grenade-Head ends up strangling me, or something, I'll make sure my dad and Uncle Kenny come round and do you over, right? And Uncle Kenny means business, I'm telling you. Like, last Christmas, he drank a whole bottle of sherry watching *Chitty-Chitty Bang-Bang* then he did this party trick where he ate a wineglass. He's hard, Uncle Kenny is. Dead hard.'

In Wallaby Springs, Bruce Doggett was trying to pull the wool over Irene's eyes by saying that Shirley was just a love-crazed psycho who kept sending him mad love-letters.

In the Plas Y Cyfoglyn Outward Bound Centre office, Barney was quizzing The Moustache about his last trip to Nepal. Whether he'd seen a Yeti, and all that stuff. In the process, he sussed out that there were 73 keys on the office wall, any one of which might or might not open the door next to the girls' washroom.

In the dormitory, Jenks was saying that he'd try and pick the lock with a paper-clip. Thankfully, I managed to dissuade him. Being Jenks, it would take thirty seconds before his finger was permanently attached to the door, and someone had to fetch a hacksaw to detach Jenks from the lock. Or Grenade-Head's fist from Jenks' face.

No, we had to go in from the outside.

'We climb up the fire-escape,' said Barney, pointing up towards the third-floor window, 'and lower Ben down on one of those ropes they've got in the lecture room for showing people how to do knots, right?'

'Me?' I complained.

Barney held up his hand. 'Don't be modest, Ben. Jenks and I will take a back seat this time. We can have the glory on another occasion. This is going to be your big moment, Kiddo.' He shook my hand. 'Besides, I'd make a much louder thud if I dropped from that height.'

Forty minutes later, I was clambering down a brick wall in pitch darkness, wearing wrap-around sunglasses and a black balaclava, with boot-polish smeared across my face and Barney's camera and Jenks' torch jammed into my back pockets.

It occurred to me that I should have sneaked Barney's camera out of his bag earlier in the day. Then I could have got one of the little kids to pose as a dead body with a bread-knife handle sticking out of it and taken a photograph. Or made some warhead gadgets out of stuck-together kitchen equipment and run off a few pictures of them. Then Barney would have got a real shock when he got the film developed.

As it was, I was about to break into a room that probably contained nothing more than sixty bottles of spare loo-cleaner and a mop. Come tomorrow, we'd have to start all over again with a new Agent Z plan.

Barney's face loomed above me. 'More rope, Corporal,' he ordered. 'Two metres to height-zero.'

'Two metres coming up, Captain,' replied Jenks.

They were right. I had to stop being sensible. I had to get into this.

'Height-zero,' I said, my feet bumping against the glass pane.

My heart began to thump. There were nuclear warheads in that room, the safety of the planet was at stake, and Agent Z needed a summer holiday in the Seychelles. I dropped onto the narrow sill and grabbed the window-frame.

'Give me slack, boys.'

The boys gave me slack. I bent down and pulled at the sash. Nothing. I should have packed the wristwatch with the diamond-edged glass-cutter and the vacuum-suckers. It was too late now. It was down to brute strength. I heaved again. The thin, metal catch broke and the sash window rocketed upwards. I plunged backwards into the darkness, opened my mouth to scream, remembered the Agent Z code of honour, didn't scream, felt the rope jerk round my chest and found myself yanked upright once more as Barney took the strain.

I gave them the all-clear sign and climbed quickly into the room before the thought of nearly having broken my neck sent my legs wibbly. I took out my torch, assumed the defence position ready for any unexpected machine-gun-fire and turned it on.

No loo-cleaner. No mop. No warheads. Just three plastic garden chairs, an old sink-unit and a filing cabinet. The warhead designs would be in there. I slid out the drawers one by one. Zilch.

I checked inside the sink unit and under the chairs for sellotaped documents. I had to take something back. The guys at MI9 knew what they were talking about. They didn't organize a stunt like this without good intelligence. Besides, they'd given Yuri the truth drug.

There was no way he could be lying about this stuff. The plans were here somewhere.

I heaved the filing cabinet away from the wall. And there it was. A small, brown, battered leather briefcase.

I retrieved it and pressed the catch. Locked. No matter. I'd take it with me. Leave it to the lab boys. Lobotomovitch could have booby-trapped it, like he booby-trapped Mandelson's hot-dog in Vienna last summer. And I didn't want to end up spread round the walls. Gingerly, I picked it up and turned back to the window.

Exitsville.

I was half way up the wall with the briefcase handle between my teeth when Jenks trod on Barney's toe. The rope giving way was a shock, but not half as big as the shock I got when I came to a violent, chest-crunching halt and found myself looking through a lighted window at Mr Lanchester reclining on a bed in stripey pyjamas reading a Jeffrey Archer novel. Potato-Head took something from his bedside drawer and began walking towards me, looking down and patting his trouser pockets.

Panic sent my biceps into overdrive. I was just above the window when it slid open. Barney and Jenks leaned over the parapet. Jenks said, 'Sorry abou . . .' and Barney whapped his mouth shut.

I winched by legs up as far as they would go and looked down. Potato-Head's balding scalp was only centimetres from my bum.

'It's just a different approach, Bob,' he said, striking a

match and lighting his fag. 'The kids see me as one of them.'

'Don't blow any of that smoke in here,' said Mr Lanchester's muffled voice, 'if you can possibly help it.'

'That's where we're different,' Potato-Head continued, chucking the match out into the dark. 'You're old-school. They do what you tell them to because they're scared of you. With me it's not like that. They respect me. I talk to them on their own level, Bob.'

I couldn't move. I was so scared I wanted to laugh. A little voice in my head told me to say, 'Yeh, Bob. He's a really street-wise dude.' Another little voice said if I so much as sniffed I'd be dead meat.

'I suppose that's why everyone goes round whistling *Oranges and Lemons*,' muttered Mr Lanchester, sarcastically.

'That's only because they didn't see you at the staff Christmas Party.' Potato-Head puffed a lungful of smoke out into the night. 'Or they'd all be taking their shirts off and standing on top of tables, singing *Rudolph the Red-Nosed Reindeer*.'

'That's enough!' snapped Mr Lanchester. 'As you well know, I was *not* drunk. The red wine simply reacted badly with my ulcer tablets.'

I gritted my teeth. There were only seconds to go before my arms conked out and I gave Potato-Head a heart-attack. I began racking my brain for simple, sensible, straightforward reasons why I might be dangling on a rope outside their bedroom window carrying a stolen briefcase.

My fingers began to uncurl. Pretend to have gone mad. It was the only option. Crash through their window and ask whether they've seen the seven-foot hamster with the shopping trolley.

I closed my eyes.

There was a knock on the bedroom door.

'Yes,' groaned Mr Lanchester. 'Come in.'

'Excuse me, Sir.' It was Barney. 'Sorry about disturbing you, it being so late and everything.'

Potato-Head glanced towards the door, glanced down at his cigarette, panicked, threw the orange butt into the night and slammed the window shut.

I went up the wall like a gecko, and hurled myself over the parapet.

'Gordon Bennet!' phewed Jenks. 'You weigh a ton, Ben. Thought I was going to have to let you go, there.'

'Thanks for hanging on,' I said. 'You're a star.'

We went to shake hands, realized we couldn't move our arms and collapsed, exhausted, onto the roof tiles. And it was only when Barney reappeared up the fire escape that I remembered the briefcase.

'Look,' I said, shoving it towards him, 'I got this.'

'No time now,' he said, lifting his shirt-cuff and checking his diving watch. 'Ben, you've got 2 minutes, forty-nine seconds to clean that polish off your face and hit the sack. So, we'd better move it. Leave the briefcase up here. We'll fetch it down later.'

'Good idea,' I agreed, heaving myself to my feet. 'Don't want it under my mattress if Lobotomovitch has done a Vienna hot-dog on the lock.'

'Sounds like you've been overdoing it a touch, Ben.' Barney patted me on the head. 'You need to get to bed and take a little rest.'

Flopsy, Diggles and Big-Boy

I was reading the bit of Mum's postcard where Dad sits on Uncle Roger's Mayflower model, when I was interrupted by Potato-Head.

He ushered me to one side, put a fatherly arm round my shoulder and said, 'Barney popped round last night. He wanted to talk about you. Now, don't be angry. He did it because he genuinely cares about you. And I promise it won't go any further than me.'

I looked back at Barney. He was drumming his fingers on his cheek and looking innocently at the ceiling like an overweight angel.

'Look. Take it from me. There's nothing wrong with missing your Mum and Dad. Especially on your first holiday away from home. And everyone gets nightmares.

Everyone cries sometimes. Even grown men. It's part of being human, Ben. Got a bit weepy myself after that crash. Kept having these horrible dreams. But . . . Like I said, I'm off duty now. So, if you're feeling down any time, you just come and knock on our door and we can have a bit of a pow-wow, yeh?'

I started to pull away from him. My hands had a pressing engagement with Barney's throat. But Potato-Head was pulling a small, beige teddy out of his pocket.

'For you.' He shoved it secretly into my jacket. 'He's called Diggles. The wife collects them. Not too keen myself. More of a model train man. But she insisted on sticking one in my suitcase. I'll just say he escaped.'

'What?!' Clearly, he'd flipped.

'It's OK. Barney told me what Justin and Gregory did to Flopsy. It was extremely mean of them. But don't worry. I'll give them the third degree about it later on today.'

'Er . . . no!' I panicked. 'Please. Don't. Don't say anything.'

'Whatever you want, Ben. Mum's the word, OK.' He thumped my back blokishly, said, 'Catch you later, Mate,' and walked off back to his fry-up.

I returned to our table and gave Barney the look of death. He shrugged his shoulders and said, 'I had to think fast, Ben, and once I'd got going, well . . . it just snowballed, you know.'

'I'm going to kill you,' I snarled.

'Go right ahead,' he said, leaning back in his chair and sipping suavely at his tea-mug. 'But if you do . . .

Remember, I won't be around to save your bacon a second time.'

I fumed. I fumed in the Land Rover. I fumed up the rocks at Capel Brechnog and fumed down again. I fumed through supper then fumed out to the jetty in case the urge to murder Barney became uncontrollable.

And sitting on the jetty was Eleanor Beasley. Crying as per usual.

'Fun place, isn't it,' I fumed, slumping down onto the wooden walkway next to her.

'I want to go home,' she said, flatly.

'Get a bus,' I suggested. 'Look pathetic and you'll probably get away without paying.'

'You don't understand,' she insisted, wiping the tear-snot from her nose with a jumper-cuff. 'I can't go home. Dad's in Germany with the army and Mum's moved in with this plonker called Darren who keeps ferrets and cactuses and has this yucky black hair all the way up his back. And he wanders round in his vest. And Dad doesn't know yet. And Gran's looking after me because I keep running away. But she's going a bit gaga and keeps calling me Sophie, but Sophie's her cat who got run over last year. And she smells a bit funny, too, Gran I mean, because she had this operation which means she pees into this plastic bag which is attached to her leg . . .'

I stopped fuming. I tried to think of something useful to say, but there wasn't anything useful to say. And then I remembered.

'Wait a tic,' I said, getting up and trotting up the hill to the Centre.

'He's called Diggles,' I said, coming back down the jetty and handing her the bear. 'For you. He . . . er . . . eats ferrets.'

She took the bear and looked at me. I smiled back and felt a warm glow of helpfulness flood through my limbs.

'Brilliant,' she hissed, 'a teddy. That's really going to help sort out my stinking family, isn't it.' She drew her arm back and launched Diggles out into the lake.

I was in the middle of thinking that I was never going to get a job as a psychiatrist when I heard a bad owl-impression from behind me. I swivelled and saw two heads poking over the edge of the centre roof.

The briefcase.

'Got to go,' I said to Eleanor. 'Put a cactus in Mr Hairyback's underpants for me, yeh?'

I headed off.

We locked the cubicle door, then checked for listening devices under the toilet seat, round the light fitting and inside the cistern. Jenks took out his Swiss army knife and we sawed our way into the briefcase.

'Decode this one for me, Brains,' whispered Barney, taking out a wad of papers and handing me a sheet covered in columns of numbers.

'Yep,' I whispered back. 'The warhead specifications disguised as a bank statement. It's an old trick. Lobotomovitch must have been getting sloppy.'

'Too right he was,' drawled Barney. 'Look at . . .'

The door hammered terrifyingly.

'Oi! How long're you going to be in there?' It was Fforbes-Giraffe. 'You can read *War and Peace* some other time. Now shift it. I'm bursting.'

Barney dropped his trousers and plonked his bum onto the toilet. 'Use the one downstairs.'

Jenks and I jumped upwards onto the rim of the loo, grabbing hold of the cistern for support.

'Oh, it's you,' moaned Fforbes-Giraffe. 'I might have known. What are you doing in there anyway, Blubber-guts? Sounds like you're moving furniture.'

Barney said nothing. I looked down. He was examining a xeroxed newspaper clipping. I rapped the top of his head to make him say something. He didn't notice. It was like rapping a log.

'Anyway,' Fforbes-Giraffe continued, 'downstairs is already occupied. So wipe your backside and get your skates on.'

I rapped Barney's head again. Slowly, his hand lifted the xeroxed sheet up towards me. It seemed to be trembling. I leant down and took the xerox from him.

'MORRISON ESCAPES FROM DARTMOOR,' ran the headline. 'Harry Morrison, who was serving a life sentence in Dartmoor high-security prison, is on the loose today after a daring roof-top escape during the early hours of yesterday morning, *writes Martin Jellicoe, our crime correspondent*. Morrison, known as 'Big-Boy' in the East-End crime community . . .' Jenks twisted the xerox so that he could read it, too . . . 'came to promi-

nence when he was arrested for his part in the Getty-Bank bullion robbery two years ago, during which three security guards were shot. His two accomplices were never apprehended despite a Europe-wide police operation. Nor was the bullion ever recovered . . .'

'I'm counting to fifty, then I'm going to climb over that door and drag you out, Wobbles.'

It didn't click at first. The guy in the photo had a beard and longer hair. But there was no mistaking. It was Grenade-Head, alright. You couldn't fake a bollard-neck and ping-pong eyeballs.

'Thirty-nine, forty, forty-one . . .'

Barney looked up at me. I did a silent whoop. This was ultramega. Agent Z had come good. And how. We were smack in the middle of a force-twelve, real-life, blood-and-guts thriller.

I glanced down. Barney was looking at me the way

you look at the family dog when it has just gone under a juggernaut. His face was Persil-white. My whoop wilted. It dawned on me that I had, indeed, gone mad. Roz was right. Grenade-Head was a genuine psycho. Worse, Jenks was right. This man was an internationally wanted, gun-toting convict.

I remembered the Wooflets and wanted suddenly to throw up.

''Ere,' whispered Jenks, pointing to the photo and grinning. 'Guess who he looks like?'

'Forty-eight, forty-nine . . .'

There was a stupendous crack. I looked up, but the cistern was still solidly attached to the wall. There was a second crack and the china toilet bowl detonated spectacularly under our weight.

My self-preservation gland went into overdrive. I shoved every sodden sheet of paper back into the briefcase, then burst open the cubicle door. The washroom was empty. Fforbes-Giraffe had fled to find a more useable, non-exploding lavatory. I paused momentarily. There were stompy, grown-up footsteps coming up the main stairwell. We had a second or two to spare.

'Move it!' I hissed to Jenks. 'Now!'

I glanced back. Barney lay on the floor, soaked in Welsh bog water, picking pieces of splintered china from his buttocks.

'Oi! What about me?' he complained.

'Think fast,' I said, shoving Jenks towards the washroom door. 'You owe me one.'

Dot-Dash-Dot-Dot-Dash-Dash

Jenks and I ran out of the Centre and down to the lake. We ducked into a clump of trees and sat down, gasping for breath.

I glanced at the small, leather briefcase sitting by my feet and, slowly, the horrifying truth began to sink in. I'd have been safer holding a large paper-bag full of plutonium.

Barney, Jenks and I were in just about as much trouble as it was humanly possible to get yourself into. Grenade-Head was an internationally-wanted criminal who wasn't too fussed about gunning down anyone who got in his way.

And we were in his way good and proper.

'Stick it back,' stammered Jenks. 'You've got to stick it

back. Then he won't know we found it . . .'

Jenks was right. Putting it back was a good idea. In theory. The problem was getting it there. I didn't want to touch the briefcase, let alone break into a third storey window holding it in my teeth. Neither did Jenks. Neither would Barney. If we were caught, it would be curtains.

We had to get rid of the thing.

OK, so he'd find out it had gone sooner or later. But he wouldn't know who'd taken it, or why. We'd still have a chance of leaving Plas Y Cyfoglyn in one piece. Better that than being found dangling outside the window of his secret room and being atomized with a single blast from a pump-action shotgun.

Inspiration hit me. 'The lake!' I shouted. 'Quick! Get some stones. We'll fill it and chuck it in the water.'

'Yeh. Yeh. Right. Good thinking,' spluttered Jenks as he began to fill the briefcase with rocks and gravel.

Some more inspiration hit me as we watched it sink below the surface. 'Evidence!' I gabbled. 'We need some evidence!'

We didn't. What we needed was a train home, and fast. But I'd watched too many late night thrillers with Dad. I strode into the water, grabbed a branch for support and fished madly. The briefcase was gone. But, as I turned back to the shore, I saw a flash of white, stuck my hand under the water and retrieved a sheet of soggy paper.

'St Dominic's Friary,' read the runny ink. 'Midnight, 13/7.'

I squeezed it as dry as I could, folded it and hid it inside my boxer shorts.

I should have thrown Jenks into the lake as well. The spoonful of oxtail hadn't reached my mouth before he was off.

'We should have put it back, Ben. I just know it. He'll find out. He'll realize someone's stolen it. He'll realize someone else knows. I'd crack. Really. If he tortured me, I'd tell. I'm not brave. I'm not like Barney . . .'

'Jenks . . . shut it,' I hissed. I didn't need this. Not now. 'Listen. He is not going to torture you. It might be twelve months before he looks in that room again. And if he does, how will he know who took the briefcase, eh?' I didn't believe a word of this stuff. I was as petrified as Jenks. But I didn't want him panicking and giving the game away. 'It might have been someone on the last course. Or the course before that. Just think about it.'

'I'm thinking about it, Ben. And what I'm thinking is, like, he shot three security guards.'

'Jenks . . .' My stomach began to go knotty and the spoon of oxtail flopped back into the bowl.

'Stop winding him up, you twerp.' It was Barney. He whacked Jenks' head and turned to me. 'What did you do with it?'

'Bottom of the lake.'

He gave me a thumbs-up. 'Nice work.'

'And you . . . ?' I asked.

He lowered his bowl and gingerly manoeuvred himself onto the chair. 'I'll pull through.'

'Who was that coming up the stairs when we scarpered?' I asked.

'Miss Jodhpurs,' Barney said, tucking into his soup.

'So . . . ?'

'She was a push-over.' Barney stuffed half a roll into his gob and chewed. 'Happens all the time, apparently. Bits of the Centre falling apart. Not enough money to keep it in good repair. She was quite apologetic about it. Anyway, I said my Dad was a big-shot lawyer and he'd just sued the Royal Opera House because this hand-rail gave way when he was finding his seat in the circle and he fell twenty feet onto some baroness who was sitting in the stalls, so Grenade-Head ought to thank his lucky stars I hadn't severed an artery.'

'And your bum?'

'Surface wounds. That's all.'

'God!' said Jenks. 'Be serious. You two think this is some kind of huge joke, don't you?'

Barney put his arm around Jenks' shoulder. 'If Grenade-Head so much as touches you, I'll send his address to Uncle Kenny, OK?'

Jenks huffed and jabbed the fork into the table-top angrily. 'See what I mean?'

'What did happen to your Uncle Kenny, by the way?' I asked. 'After he ate that wineglass?'

'He had to go into hospital, of course,' grumped Jenks. 'What the hell do you think happens after you eat a wineglass?'

'Oh, right,' I said. 'Did they have to operate?'

'Nah. They just gave him a laxative and some painkillers, then sent him to see a shrink.'

Jenks was right, of course. It was serious. I was just trying not to think about how serious it was. We'd probably get home without being chopped up and put into tins, but that wasn't the point. Like Barney said, we had another problem on our hands. We knew Grenade-Head's secret. We had to do something.

'Just ring the police, you dumbos,' Jenks said.

Barney wasn't so sure. If they came in, guns blazing, and dragged Grenade-Head back to Dartmoor, fine. But if, on the other hand, they just came and sniffed around, well, Grenade-Head would realize something was up, and might just decide to do some sniffing of his own.

Besides, who was going to believe three kids with nothing but a soggy piece of paper?

The soggy piece of paper!

I extracted it from my underwear and showed it to Barney. 'A secret meeting?' I suggested.

'Thirteenth of the seventh,' he read. 'That's this Friday . . . Or maybe the 13 of July last year. Or the year before that. Or next year. Pff!' He dropped the sheet onto the table. 'Maybe it's about something else altogether. Maybe it's some orienteering guff. Maybe he goes out with the Capel Curig Bat-Watching group. Maybe he was meeting his Aunt Dora for a midnight picnic. Who knows?'

We talked and talked and talked. And the longer we talked the stupider it sounded. An escaped bullion-robber running an outward-bound centre? It was crazy.

They all scarpered to Rio de Janeiro, didn't they? No. It was his brother in the photograph. Or the picture just looked like him, and someone had given it to him as a joke.

There had to be some simple explanation.

And if there wasn't? If Grenade-Head really was Harry Morrison? Well, Agent Z was a big-time operator, sure. But not this big. Get carried away with the heroics and we could end up looking like Irene, with 37 tubes up our noses. Or worse.

We took a decision. We'd let it go, keep our heads down and stay out of trouble until the end of the week. Then we could hand the whole thing over to the grown-ups when we were out of harm's way.

And then we could sell our story to the *Daily Mail*.

If there was any story to tell.

There was a story to tell.

It was the following night. I'd climbed into bed and was on the verge of falling asleep when I heard the opening bars of *Heartbreak Hotel* being played outside the window. I thought, at first, that I'd started dreaming already, but the tune continued even when I sat up. I went over to the window and threw up the sash.

The tune stopped and I heard a brief scurrying in the dark. Then nothing.

'Weird or what?' I said, as Barney leant on the sill next to me.

'Yeh. They've heard of Elvis, even here,' he mumbled. 'Anyway, I'm off back to bye-byes.'

'Suppose so . . .' I said. And then I saw it. 'No, wait, Barney. Look,' I insisted, pointing out into the night.

Barney looked. 'So what. There's a flashing light on the far side of the lake. Very good, Ben. You can have your Brownie Observation Badge in the morning.'

'Wassappening?' Jenks said, waking up. He jumped out of bed onto an upturned belt-buckle, yelped, crashed into Captain Prat's bed and wandered over.

'No,' I said to Barney. He was wrong. I knew it. 'There's nothing on the far side of the lake. Remember? Just trees and . . . more trees. Besides, there . . .! See how it goes on and off? It's like a message, or something.'

'I think you're right,' said Captain Prat, who had toddled over to see what all the fuss was about. 'It's the rescue craft from Planet Moron finally come to take you lot home.' And with that he turned and stalked back to his bed.

'Barney . . . ?' I asked. 'What do you reckon . . . ?'

'Shhh!'

'Hey! What're you doing . . . ?' Jenks squealed.

'Shut up and keep still,' hissed Barney.

I turned to see him biroing dots and dashes onto Jenks' arm, stopping every few seconds to stare out into the darkness.

The light seemed to flash forever. By the time it stopped, Jenks looked like The World's Most Tattooed Boy.

'Right. Beddy-byes,' said Barney, putting the biro back into his pyjamas. 'And Jenks . . . ?'

'What?'

'I realize the chance is one in ten million, but do remember not to have a shower before breakfast, yeh?'

Next morning, we went into the lecture room and began trawling through the bookshelves. *The Survival Guide, Outward Bound!*, *The Wilderness Encyclopaedia*, *The Collins Guide to British Mammals*, *Me and My Tent*.

We tried everything. But no luck.

And only then did Jenks remember that the morse code was printed down the side of his torch. We hot-tailed it back upstairs, dug out the torch, rolled Jenks' sleeve up and waited for Barney to finish the translation.

Jenks' arm read, '. . .ing madnight this frigoy. St Diminicx. Meedint nadnigst zhis griday. St Gominics. Merting midnighf tois fridag. Dt Domifics. Meetiny midsight thid Friday. St Dominids.'

Jenks said that the guy operating the flashlight must have been dyslexic. Barney said Jenks had wriggled too much. Either way, we got the message. It was this Friday. Not next year, or last year, or the year before. And if it was Grenade-Head's Aunt Dora arranging another picnic, she didn't want anyone else coming along to share the sandwiches.

'It's like this,' Barney whispered, as we waited outside the bathroom for Jenks to shower off the clue. 'We go to this place. We hide in a tree or something and take photos with the automatic zoom lens attachment on my camera, then . . .'

'Where, Barney? Go where?'

'St Dominic's.'

'Which is . . . ?'

'Ah,' said Barney. 'You're a bright lad, Ben. I'll give you that.'

I had a funny feeling that the location of St Dominic's Friary wasn't going to be in *The Collins Guide to British Mammals* either.

We were hunched over an Ordnance Survey map of the area, digesting our treacle tart, when Roz appeared.

'Planning your escape, chaps?'

'We're not doing anything at all,' said Jenks.

'Ah, right,' she replied, tapping the side of her nose and winking. 'Need any help?'

'It's Ben's great-grandad,' said Barney, leaning nonchalantly back in his chair and putting his hands behind his head. 'He was in the church. Some sort of Friar-type. You know, the big robes and the funny hairstyle and stuff. Used to be at a place called St Dominic's. Somewhere round here, we reckon. Ben's mum said she'd really like a photo of the place, or a postcard or something.'

Roz put her head on one side and gave Barney an extremely sceptical look. 'How come he became a great-grandad? They don't really go in for having kids in monasteries, do they?'

'Ah, no. Indeed not,' said Barney, fumbling for a micro-second. 'Bit of a dark family secret, really. Ben's great-gran used to deliver the milk from the farm down the road. They got caught having a snog in the cloister and had to elope together.' Barney smiled, having got

back into his stride. 'Ended up running a bike-shop in Barnstaple, apparently.'

Roz raised her eyebrows and smiled. 'Very interesting.' She then leant forward, plonked her finger in the middle of the map and said, 'There's a ruined abbey called St Dominic's . . . just there. Right next to the big waterfall. It was one of the places we had to go to when we were orienteering. Mind you, according to the National Trust sign, it fell into ruins about four hundred years ago. But perhaps your great-grandad was very, very young when he was snogging milkmaids.' She turned and plodded off. 'Ciao, Kiddywinks.'

'Er . . . Excuse me.' I cleared my throat and stood up to my full height so as to look sensible and adult. 'This is going to sound really stupid, but . . .'

The large, bearded constable put down his coffee, removed his glasses and leant lazily on the counter. I had to move fast. Lesley would be back at the car in five minutes. A fraction too long in here and I'd have to explain why I was buying a refill for an asthma inhaler in the police station.

'I'm not really sure where to start . . .' I flustered.

'Right at the beginning,' suggested the constable, sipping his coffee and relaxing himself ready for a long story. 'Always the best place in my opinion.'

'Well . . . Years ago there was this big robbery. These thieves stole loads of gold from a place called the Getty-Bank. And one of them was called Harry Morrison.'

'Rings a bell,' he said, inserting a biro into his right ear to clean out the wax. 'Go on.'

'And he was the only one who got caught. Except that he escaped, from Dartmoor, right . . .'

'Right . . .'

I took a deep breath. 'He's here. He's running the Outward Bound Centre. Ed Michaels. Ed Michaels is Harry Morrison.'

I was right. It did sound stupid. I had been really convincing in front of the washroom mirror. But now, here, standing in front of a burly policeman stirring ear-wax into his coffee with a biro, I sounded completely whacko.

'We found this briefcase in a locked room in the Centre. It had press clippings and photos inside. And these bank statements. And this note about a meeting at a place called St Dominic's up in the hills. And we saw this morse code message being flashed across the lake last night about the meeting and . . .'

Barney was right. Constable Ear-Wax was not going to raid the Centre, guns blazing. He wasn't going to move from the counter if he could possibly help it.

He nodded slowly. 'Anything else?'

'Well, no, I mean, like, that's it.'

'An escaped leopard on the run from Porthmadog Zoo? Little green men with bobbly antennae wotsits getting out of flying saucers and saying, 'Take me to your leader'? A couple of nuns robbing Barclays with sawn-off shotguns?'

'I . . .' I could feel my cheeks glowing like toaster elements.

'Let's just leave it, shall we, young man,' he suggested. 'Call it a day. You've had your fun. Now run along and we'll say nothing more about it.'

'Sorry, Barney,' I said. 'I just had to. This thing is scaring the pants off me. We can't just go out and nab these people on our own. We're not Sherlock Holmes.'

'Just one thing, Ben,' said Barney.

'What?'

'Keep your fingers crossed that your policeman isn't being paid off by Grenade-Head to keep quiet. Then things could really start hotting up round here.'

My stomach did gymnastics.

Crocodiles on Steroids

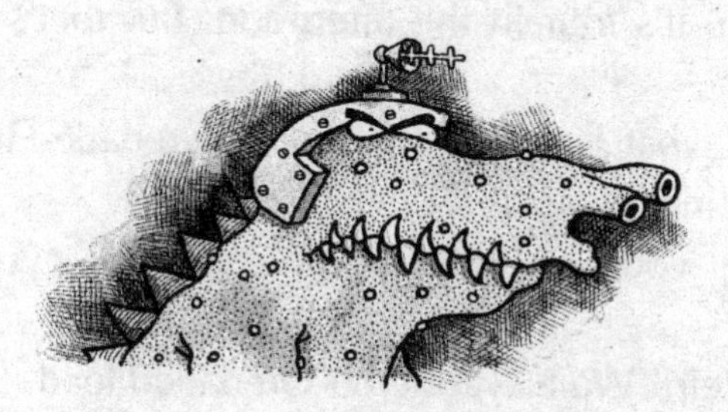

Grenade-Head had enough time to scream, that was all.

One moment, he was standing on the rocky outcrop, grinning to himself and watching the bodies of Nosher and Sugs as they were gobbled up by the white water one hundred metres below. The next he was dangling face-down over the edge of the precipice, watching those same rapids foaming angrily beneath him.

He twisted his head skywards. His ankle was in the grip of a gruesome, horned claw. A head appeared. A head like nothing he'd seen before, even in his worst nightmares. Steaming nostril-slime. Teeth like a rack of butcher's knives. A five-ton crocodile on steroids.

'Hello Mr Morrison,' growled the cyberlizard.

'What . . . ? No . . . ! I must be dreaming . . .' gasped Grenade-Head.

'Crikey, these humans are so stupid,' said the raptoid, turning to its partner who had just lumbered up the brink of the ravine. It glanced down at Grenade-Head once more. 'Of course you're not dreaming, you brainless little man. It's four in the afternoon. But that's not the point.'

'Er . . . what is the point?' asked Grenade-Head, his brain reeling.

'Killing you, of course,' grunted the cyberlizard casually.

'No! Help! Wait!' yabbered Grenade-Head. 'Wait!'

'What now?' grumped the raptoid. 'Get it off your chest. And make it snappy. I can't hang around all day. We've still got a headmistress to finish off before tea-time.'

'The bullion!' Grenade-Head shouted. 'I'll tell you where the bullion is. You can have it. All of it. I won't argue.'

'Pfff!' huffed the cyberlizard, spraying Grenade-Head with a thick overcoat of acid snot. 'No can do, Big-Boy. We've got it already. Probably half-way to Zenon Nine by now. I'll be cashing it in tomorrow morning, then getting the builders to start on the Olympic swimming pool I've been promising the kids all summer . . .'

'For goodness sake,' moaned the second raptoid. 'Stop dithering and finish him off, will you.'

'Gnkgh!' Grenade-Head kicked and twizzled. 'Kghffh!'

'OK,' muttered the first cyberlizard. 'Enough chat. Got to be off, Mr Morrison. Have a nice day, as you people say.'

The raptoid let go and stood up. Grenade-Head's ear-piercing scream faded slowly away. There was a distant 'flump!', like a sack of potatoes hitting the front of an express train. Then nothing, just the churning of the rapids.

The cyberlizard brushed the dirt and grass from its warty leather rib-cage and turned to its companion. 'What repulsive little animals. Just because they've got ABS braking systems, they think they run the whole damn universe. Anyway, give me a direction-readout for this Block woman . . .'

If only.

I was a mess. Suppressed panic and creeping horror had turned my brain into sludge. I couldn't eat properly. I couldn't sleep properly. I fell out of a stationary canoe without being pushed. Barney began biting his nails and Jenks had a revolting flare-up of the nervous eczema which he hadn't suffered from since he got into the Renault while his Dad was working in Sheffield last summer, hit reverse and took out most of the new extension.

It was four days until Grenade-Head's rendezvous.

The 13th of July fell smack in the middle of the big trek we had timetabled for the end of the course: a three-day expedition-job where we got dumped in the middle of nowhere with a sealed envelope of directions, and had to find our way by the stars, trap wild boars, cook them over open fires, knit tents out of bullrushes, drink our own wee and somehow get back to the Centre in one piece. The usual Outward Bound stuff.

Precisely what we were going to do at midnight on Friday, I didn't know. Barney kept saying, 'I'm working on it, Ben,' but he didn't seem as confident as usual, and if he carried on the way he was going, he'd have no fingers left to do it when it happened.

That evening, I made the mistake of writing Mum and Dad a card while sitting next to Fforbes-Giraffe and Captain Prat in the games room. They saw what I was doing and nicked the card so that they could read it out to everyone for a good laugh.

It took them four microseconds to realize that my handwriting was the same as the handwriting on the fake love-letters from Penny Threadgold. By the end of the fifth microsecond, I was being dragged into the empty kitchens and duffed over. I hardly bothered to defend myself. Compared to what might happen on Friday night, this was kids' stuff, hardly worth worrying about. Besides, if I ended up in casualty, that was fine by me. The further away from Grenade-Head the better.

My nose was bleeding like a special effect from *Rocky IV* when Mel Carver and Jackie Phipps put their heads round the door to find out what the noise was. Either they felt sorry for me, or they wanted to make the point that girls could do this sort of thing, too. They rolled up their sleeves and got stuck in. I left them to it and crawled away to the nearest loo-roll to try and stop myself bleeding to death.

At supper, Captain Prat looked like he'd been beaten around the head with a frying pan, which he probably had.

Later that same night, The Moustache was woken by the mating-yowl of a deranged tomcat. He had shooshed it away down the drive and was going back through the main doors when he saw Babs and Penny climbing off the back of two large motorbikes. Penny tried to explain that Dai and Tony (the young chaps with the sideburns) had very kindly given them a lift back to the Centre after they'd got desperately lost while out for an evening stroll. But Babs blew it when she noticed The Moustache, said, 'Hey, Pen, look at those two funny men in dressing gowns,' hiccuped loudly and passed out face-first on the gravel.

They were confined to their rooms for a day, along with The Incredible Hulk.

Egged on by Winston, he had called the office from the payphone in the entrance hall and asked to speak to Mr Dawson. When Potato-Head picked up the receiver, the Hulk slipped into his Breezeblock voice and said, 'I'm afraid I've got some rather bad news for you, Mr Dawson. Sorry to trouble you while you're on holiday, but I thought it best to tell you at the earliest possible opportunity. I've just had a rather peculiar letter from a Doctor Brightwell at the hospital. He was very apologetic, but there was, it seems, an unexplained mix-up in surgery after your accident. Apparently, one of the nursing staff has found the top half of your ear in one of their fridges. He says there is no reason to panic at the moment . . .'

It was quite a good joke, but not half as good as the fact that Mr Lanchester was passing through the entrance hall at the time. He stood behind the Incredible Hulk and waited until he had reached the end of his little monologue. Then he hoiked him off the ground by his shirt-collar.

Potato-Head was in the process of squeezing his bandage to see whether it was empty when the Incredible Hulk's throttled scream came down the phone. It was so blood-curdling that Potato-Head completely forgot about his ear and assumed Breezeblock was having a heart-attack. He was only prevented from ringing 999 on her behalf by Mr Lanchester's rapid appearance in the office.

Meanwhile, Down Under, John Goolagong of the Wallaby Springs police had arrested Irene when he found her waiting outside Shirley's flat armed with a sheep syringe and a naily plank. Brad Toomey had surfed into a Portuguese Man O' War and taken over Irene's hospital bed. And Mandy, the plain swot who lived with the old bat Auntie Doris, had finally taken off her pink-rimmed glasses and let down her plaited hair to get snogged by Wayne.

'Jeez, you're a real bute, Mand!' he gasped.

Up in the hills, we learnt how to catch fish with a safety pin and a piece of string. We learnt how to con-

struct a rope bridge across a stream. We learnt how to make a stretcher for an injured person out of two branches and three jumpers, and how to carry them down a mountain without them popping their clogs.

What we didn't have were classes in relaxation, self-defence and al-fresco stake-out techniques.

Barney tried to cheer us up by organizing some under-cover operations for Agent Z. We emptied 46 tea-bags, filled them with soap-powder, glued them back together again and biroed micro-Zs in the corner of each bag.

We carved pieces of driftwood into two long, horned claws, pressed a string of tracks into the muddy shore of the lake, then watched The Moustache run off three colour films to send to the Royal Ornithological Society.

Just before bedtime one evening, Barney gathered a large group of young kids in the games room and told them a long, complex and truly stomach-churning ghost story about The Severed Hand of Plas Y Cyfoglyn. Meanwhile, upstairs, Jenks and I blew up eight flesh-coloured rubber gloves which we'd found in the store-room and squeezed them tightly into every zip-top wash-bag we could find.

We tried hard. But our hearts weren't in it. Friday was getting closer. And it had big teeth.

'No way,' said Jenks. 'I don't want anything to do with it. You can have my Z badge back. There. Take it. I don't care. You two want your brains testing. You're sick in the head, that's what you are.'

Barney put his hands in his pockets and stared into the distance. 'This isn't about Agent Z, Jenks. This is something else altogether. This is about honour, and pride, and duty, and doing what is right. This is going to be something to tell your grandchildren about.'

At which point, two unpleasant and sinister facts became suddenly clear to me.

One: something had gone profoundly wrong somewhere deep inside Barney's brain. We'd been fantasizing for too long. Agent Z. The silver-foil flight-deck in the command centre. Lobotomovich's hot-dog. The Severed Hand. Barney's reality-meter had finally blown a gasket. He couldn't tell the difference between life and play-acting. This was just another game to him.

Two: I couldn't do anything about it, short of knocking him unconscious and roping him to the seat of an overnight train for Aberdeen. Barney changed his mind like other people changed their kneecaps. He was going to plunge off into the woods in the middle of Friday night in search of a man who had escaped from a high-security prison. And what's more, I'd end up going with him. I just knew it. He could persuade you to stand stark naked on one leg in the middle of the playground with a traffic cone on your head if he reckoned it was worth the effort.

I thought about breaking one of his toes while he was asleep. But if Potato-Head or Lanchester found out, I'd spend the next three years visiting the school psychologist.

I tried to persuade the Incredible Hulk to impersonate Barney's mum on the phone and order him back for Great-Aunt Winifred's unexpected funeral. But the Incredible Hulk's Dorset accent sounded like Martian, and he was fighting shy of hoax phonecalls for the time being.

I even considered poison. And then I remembered the Sunday afternoon last term when Kev Baxter bet Barney he couldn't eat the entire contents of Kev's mum's fridge. Kev lost ten weeks' paper-round wages, six of which went on restocking the fridge. No. Give Barney a plate of Arsenic Lasagne, and he'd be back for seconds in five minutes and asking whether he could have the recipe.

There was no way out. We were headed right up Cow-Pat Creek, and we didn't have a paddle between us.

'The two of us are having a grand old time here in Blakeney,' wrote Mum, on Postcard Number 2. 'The other day your Dad was chatting to Mr Blenkinsop from the caravan next door, and Geoff (that's Mr Blenkinsop) said, seeing as how we're a bit cramped with Gwen and Roger, we could borrow their caravan when they left.

'So, we've got a caravan all to ourselves now. That means Roger can put his Mayflower model back together in peace. Dad can put his feet on the sofa. And I can watch *Wallaby Springs*. Plus, we won't have to take Badger to the local vet again (did I tell you about him getting attacked by those awful cats?). I must say, the Blenkinsops' caravan is a cut above Gwen's. It's got a TV and a video and a cassette player. And there's a couple of mountain bikes outside that we can use, too.

'Yesterday we hired a powerboat and went out to see the seal sanctuary at the end of the point. Today we're off to Cromer to learn sailboarding. We've hardly seen Gwen and Roger for the past three days . . .'

There was more, but I didn't want to read it. I didn't want to know how much fun I might have had if Barney hadn't bribed 3B. Besides, Mum's handwriting had gone ultra-micro and my eyes were hurting. I turned the card over. On the front was a picture of the Bar-Tailed Godwit, which was a bit of a star attraction at the Blakeney Point Bird Reserve, according to the blurb.

I got out my marker pen, gave the godwit a pair of impossibly large feet, added a large Z to its chest plumage and stuck it to the noticeboard in the entrance hall.

I bumped into Grenade-Head when I was passing the office on Wednesday morning.

'How's it going, young man?' he asked.

'Er . . .' I goggled stupidly at his huge, sinewy hands and couldn't help imagining them wrapped around the handle of a pump-action shot-gun. 'Yes, thank you . . . Fine, I mean.'

'Great,' he grinned. 'Glad to see you're getting along with those other two boys, by the way. You seem to be the best of friends, now. What did I tell you? Team spirit. Works wonders.'

'Yep.' I pressed myself against the corridor wall.

'Looking forward to the trek tomorrow?' he asked.

I forced my head to nod.

'Good. Can't wait, myself. Get out there into the hills at night. Wonderful. I think it's going to be most . . . profitable. Yes. Most profitable.' He paused. 'And after that, I shan't be seeing any of you again.'

'Where are you going?' I spluttered idiotically, without thinking.

The ping-pong eyes bulged at me quizzically, and my guts arranged themselves into a reef-knot.

'I'm not going anywhere,' he said, slowly. 'You're going home, remember?'

'Oh, yes. Sure. Brilliant. Anyway, got to go.'

I ran.

The Sacred Box of Australian Midgets

It was Thursday morning. The start of the big trek. The Greens, Reds, Yellows and Blues were all limbering up, getting ready to follow the Pole Star and drink wee. Back in the Centre, Grenade-Head was probably oiling his Colt 45 and selecting the spade he would use to dig up the bullion before heading into the sun.

We were waiting for the arrival of the Greens' personalized Land Rover when Potato-Head caught sight of a small, brown head bobbing in the water under the jetty and went to investigate. When he returned, it was clear that Diggles was not in good shape.

'Ben,' he said, squeezing a litre of slimey, green water out of the bedraggled, furry body, 'if you didn't want him, you could just have given him back, you know.

You didn't have to go and do this.'

'Ah . . . Sorry about that,' I blithered. One of Diggles' legs had gone. Pike-lunch, probably. 'He just sort of . . . ran off.' I smiled weakly. 'They've got minds of their own, haven't they?'

But Potato-Head had already turned and begun walking away, up the path to the Centre to find an empty radiator for the sodden animal.

'What on earth was that all about?' asked Jenks, turning to me and knotting his eyebrows.

'It's a personal thing,' I said. 'He doesn't like to talk about it.'

Forty minutes later, the Land Rover puttered away leaving us standing on a hillock in the middle of nowhere. Captain Prat opened the large, buff envelope and read out the instructions for Leg No. 1. Eleanor did the compass business and we struck out 21 degrees North North West.

The line of walkers fell gradually silent. Soon you could hear nothing apart from the sound of gravel crunching under leather boots and the hissing of wind on rock. The ground rose and the vegetation began to thin out. Here and there, the scrub was dotted with the blackened stumps of dead trees, the only remains of the forests that once covered this land completely.

We were entering The Empty Quarter.

The yellow grass gave way to cold, grey stone. We clambered across the ridge of boulders and an endless chain of distant mountains loomed into view. The huge space made me feel dizzy and nervous. But the wind was clean and cold. I took a chance and unstrapped my face-mask. The air tasted wonderful.

Our last week in the city kept coming back to me. The howling of the dog-packs roaming the dirty streets. Sporadic gunfire. The blocks down by the river burning for three days. Then, after the fires, the vultures turning slowly in the columns of smoke.

No-one else had believed Ziggy's story about the Mountain People. They said it was just too good to be true. Ziggy had gone mad, they reckoned. It wasn't uncommon. The city sent people crazy all the time.

But I believed him. I still had the tattered, ancient, single volume of the *Encyclopaedia Brittanica* (*Pim – Rog*) which Grandad Hammond had given me the day before he died. I had seen the pictures and read the words underneath them. So I knew Ziggy was right. There really were such things as Peru and quiches and radioactivity. There really were things called pullovers which were woven from the outsides of animals called sheep. There really were such things as records, which made a sound called Elvis Presley when you traced a needle around their grooves.

Ziggy had told me many stories about the months he had spent with the Mountain People. But most of all, it was his description of the Sacred Box of Australian Midgets which had stuck in my mind. I used to dream about it night after night after night.

The ceremony happened every full moon, apparently. They would sit in a semicircle, all three hundred of them, men, women and children. The Arch-Priest would call for silence and two men would place the Holy Box in front of the people. The Arch-Priest's assistant would then begin pedalling the trizzerty-generata. The Arch-Priest would take the Hallowed Cassette from its velvet-lined case and slide it into the mouth of the Holy Box. Suddenly, the window on the box would light up and everyone was able to see the Australian Midgets running around inside saying things like, 'Reckon you could drop in on your way home, Bruce? Sheila's Siamese has got the runs again,' and, 'Hi, Shirl! Rustle me up a cappucino, would you, babe? My throat's as dry as a camel's toupé.' And everyone would laugh themselves stupid at the antics of the little electronic people running around inside the black box.

Half an hour later, when the tape finished, the Arch-Priest would open one of the Blessed Cans of Alice Springs Export Lager. Everyone would take a sip, say 'G-day!' to the person sitting next to them and pass it on . . .

'Listen up, Ben,' said Barney, rudely butting into my fantasy, 'I've been doing a little homework. Now, obviously, it's going to be dark at this meeting of theirs. So, if I use the flash, we're going to be done for. But, wait for this . . . I've nicked four safety flares from the stores.' He patted his rucksack. 'You light these and throw them and they can illuminate a whole mountainside. So, we won't need a flash. And if we chuck it far enough, they won't have a clue about where we . . . Ben, where the hell are you?'

'3067 AD,' I explained carefully. 'The whole planet has been destroyed by pollution, and civilization has fallen apart and no-one knows what a video is any more and I'm on this expedition to find the Mountain People who have got this freaky, white skin and freaky, white hair because they hid deep inside their tunnels with their chickens and pigs and things during The Dark Days when there was too much radiation . . . and I'm having a really good time, if you don't mind.'

'Sounds cool,' said Barney, wandering ahead. 'Give us a call when you're back in the present, OK?'

I carried on walking. High on a ridge to my left, I could see one of the Mountain People's outriders, sitting astride his armoured sheep, wearing his long, chicken-skin robe. I remembered something Ziggy had said and began to sweat. These people didn't like strangers.

It was at precisely this point that Potato-Head stopped to take a look at the map. It turned out that we were going in completely the wrong direction. Captain Prat called Eleanor a 'dribbling thickhead', Eleanor called Captain Prat 'stuck-up little bogey', Potato-Head calmed everyone down, and pointed the line of walkers 21 degrees South South East.

I hadn't noticed any of this. I was just dodging a sharpened pig-bone javelin hurled from the ridge when I walked smack into Penny Threadgold who was striding back towards me. She got a splendid, purple bruise on her chin. I got an eyeful of lipstick and a headache.

It was clear by now that Fforbes-Giraffe and Captain Prat were leading the expedition. I wasn't bothered. Like Mum said, I was going to do something sensitive and artistic when I grew up, so I didn't need the training in leadership skills. Fforbes-Giraffe and Captain Prat, on the other hand, were going to be chairmen of ICI, or directors of the Bank of England, so they needed lots of practice in giving orders and sitting on their backsides while other people did all the work.

Besides, the work was fun.

Jenks got to climb between two overhanging tree-tops and knit a commando-style rope bridge that held everyone's weight except Potato-Head's. Barney got to lead the rescue party down into the ravine and haul Potato-Head up again. And I got to pick the gravel out of Potato-Head's leg-wound with my penknife tweezers before bandaging it up.

On the far side of the ravine, there was a fleet of canoes waiting for us. We climbed aboard and paddled five miles downstream until we saw the flappy, pink orienteering doo-dah on the left bank. We beached the boats and headed up a hill so steep I began to wish I had actually bought an asthma inhaler refill to stop Barney wheezing and gasping.

We sat on the summit and ate spam sandwiches. The fruit from the bottom of Potato-Head's rucksack, which had helped cushion his fall so well, was somewhat runny now, so we skipped it and stuck to the Penguins.

During the afternoon, I was tortured mercilessly by the Mountain People who then chained me up in a security tunnel. Barney almost persuaded Penny that, when she returned to the Centre with 18 Bacardi and Cokes inside her, she had got up in the middle of the night and run round the corridors stark naked before Lesley put her to bed again. The Mountain People finally let me go when I cured their pig's appendicitis with daring surgical techniques I remembered from the *Encyclopaedia Brittanica* (*Pim – Rog*). And Jenks totally destroyed my favourite pair of boxer shorts coming down one particularly flinty slope on his bum.

I used a *lot* of disinfectant.

We pitched camp on the shore of a mountain lake. When we'd dumped our rucksacks, Potato-Head treated himself to a public cigarette, Penny attempted to cover her bruise with foundation cream, Jenks put our tent together, Roz took it apart and put it together again properly, Barney excavated his belly-button to start a fire, and I built a latrine.

I dug out a pit between two rocks, and balanced a comfy seat-log over the hole. I strung a loo-roll from a bendy twig and carved the words 'Now Wash Your Hands' onto a piece of driftwood.

My assignment finished, I pottered off along the water's edge and sat myself down on a boulder. I was in the middle of piloting an imaginary gyrocopter down the valley when I was interrupted by a Wonder of Nature. Hearing a flurry of wings above me, I looked up to see a huge bird of prey plunge down into the grass at the edge of the lake. There was a scuffle and the terrified squeak of something small and furry kicking the bucket. The bird rose again, more slowly this time. Dangling from its talons was a freshly killed rabbit.

It struck me that this would really have appealed to Ted Hughes.

I was just composing the opening lines of 'Talon-Death Attack' when I was interrupted by a Horror of Nature. A large stone whizzed over my head towards the flapping bird. Seconds later, Captain Prat and Fforbes-Giraffe plunged past me shouting and clapping their hands. Fforbes-Giraffe bent down, picked up another stone and wanged it into the air. The bird executed a neat swerve, realized it was outgunned, dropped the rabbit and flew off to find something else to murder. The wazzocks waded into the water and recovered the bunny-corpse.

I made a mental note to remind myself not to send my

own children to public school when I was rich and grown-up.

Back at the camp, Potato-Head said it would be much more sensible to stick to the packet soup, but Fforbes-Giraffe and Captain Prat were insistent. This was what Outward Bound was all about, they said. Potato-Head gave in and let them cook the rabbit. It'd probably come in handy when there was nothing left in the Managing Director's snack-fridge at ICI and they had to cook one of the secretaries over an open fire for brunch.

They sliced the head off and started skinning the creature. Eleanor wandered over and asked what was for supper. Fforbes-Giraffe turned to her and grinned. A metre of rabbit gizzard slithered off his lap onto her walking boots. She did not have a very strong stomach. But to her credit, when she was sick she did manage to do it down Fforbes-Giraffe's back.

'I sneaked a look at Captain Prat's envelope during supper,' said Barney, popping a stack of five Polos into his mouth. 'The route's perfect. Tomorrow night, we're going to be camping about three miles away from St Dominic's. The friary is in the middle of a big pine forest. Slow going in the dark, but we can do it in, say, forty minutes, I reckon. We can be out and back within two hours, and no-one will be any the wiser. Grenade-Head and his cronies'll probably approach on the old track that connects the ruin to the main road. It'll be dark, so there's no reason for them to come through the woods. All we have to do is keep our heads down and stay in the trees. It'll be a doddle.'

'Uh-huh,' I said.

'Bip! Bip! Peeong! Bip!' went Battlestar II, as Jenks atomized asteroid no. 563.

'Come on, Jenks,' grouched Barney. 'I need you with me on this one. The planning has to be perfect. We can't afford a cock-up.'

'I'm not coming,' said Jenks. 'I told you. I'm not coming.'

'Just imagine it,' said Barney, staring into the night. 'The front page of the *Chronicle*. "Local Boys Help Capture Bullion Robbers." We'll be famous, Jenks . . .'

'Peeong! Peeong! Peeong! Bip!' went Battlestar II.

'. . . A few phonecalls and we could probably wangle a slot on breakfast TV,' Barney continued. 'The big time . . .'

'I'm sorry about your teddy bear, Ben,' said a squeaky voice.

I looked up. It was Eleanor.

'Your teddy bear? Flopsy?' said Barney, looking confused. 'So you really do have a teddy bear. Weird. I must be psychic.'

'Diggles,' I replied. 'He was called Diggles. And he wasn't mine. He was Potato-Head's. His wife gave it to him to keep him company on holiday.'

'The one he fished out of the lake this morning?' asked Jenks.

I nodded. Eleanor put her hand over her mouth and blushed. 'Oh . . . I'm sorry . . . I hope he wasn't really cross . . . Look . . . I just wanted to say . . . thanks. You know. For letting me moan at you and all.'

'What's the matter?' asked Barney.

'It's a long story,' I said, on Eleanor's behalf.

'Take a seat, kid,' replied Barney, 'and help yourself to a Polo. Now give us the low-down.'

When she finished repeating her long and sorry story, I looked at Barney expecting him to say something useful and mature. But it was Jenks who spoke.

'Sounds like a pretty normal family to me.' He picked his nose and flicked the contents out into the darkness. 'My mum ran off once. Four months. It was awful. Not that I blame her, like. I mean, the week before she ran off, Kevin's room fell into the lounge because he and Chris were playing trampolines on the bed. And Cheryl was being anorexic and Dad'd accidentally reversed the van over the dog when he was backing out of the drive. And it was her birthday, too, and everyone had completely forgotten. And she met this old boyfriend from school while she was queueing up in the post office to cash the child benefit thing and his wife had just left him. And he was just getting a visitor's passport 'cos he was going to the South of France to get this building job with a mate doing up old farmhouses. And the two of them got talking over a coffee and, well, to put it in a nutshell, she said, what the hell, and they were on a ferry by teatime, 'cos she's like that, you know, spur of the moment and everything. And we didn't really notice she'd gone until we found Dad sitting on the stairs crying one morning. And he was in a real mess 'cos she'd just left this note saying how she couldn't stand it any more and how we never took any notice of her and Dad thought she'd gone and done herself in, but we got this postcard the next week . . .'

'God, that's awful,' said Eleanor.

'Yeh, but she came back eventually. She said she missed us. When she'd finally stopped hating us, that is. And besides, this guy only had this pokey little caravan with a roof which leaked and France wasn't very sunny in November. But she stuck it out for two months, like, to prove her point. And she was really chuffed when she got back because there were about four million Guinness cans in the back bathroom and there was this bright green fungus on the top of the cooker which meant that everything had fallen apart without her. And she made us clean it all up and cooked us all this slap-up meal and we bought her a new dog, called Splodge, as a kind of late birthday present to make up for Spot's being flattened and everything. And she thought he was brilliant, except he climbed onto the kitchen table before we got round to dessert and ate all the crumble and knocked this bottle onto the floor and it smashed. And Wayne ran in in his bare feet and couldn't walk for days . . .'

I was just watching Eleanor's gloomy face break into a tiny, horrified smile when Barney tapped me on the shoulder and beckoned me away.

'True love,' he said as we walked back up the grassy slope, 'best leave them to it. Anyway . . . about tomorrow night. You're coming with me, Ben, aren't you? You're not going to leave your old mate in the lurch?'

'I must be insane,' I said, knowing there was no

choice.

'Don't worry,' he said, gripping my shoulder in a manly way. 'Sir Francis Drake, Edmund Hillary, Nelson, Alexander Graham Bell . . . They were all a bit insane. It's a necessary part of being brave and fearless.

'Alexander Graham Bell?' I said. 'What's brave and fearless about inventing the telephone?'

'That's irrelevant, Ben,' he replied, breaking his last Polo in two and handing me the smaller piece. 'What I'm talking about, is . . .'

'Brrpthrrrrpplopbulrbplop . . .!' gargled someone, or something, from the nearby undergrowth.

'What the . . . ?' I looked towards the trees. It sounded like one of our team members was being throttled by the Severed Hand of Plas Y Cyfoglyn.

We ran over and peered round a large, protective shrub. The noise was coming from Captain Prat. He was doubled over on the comfy seat-log above my carefully dug latrine-pit. Potato-Head had been right. The packet soup had been the best bet by a long chalk. Bunnikins had not agreed with the cricket captain, and was making a fast exit from both ends of him at the same time.

'Nature gets her own back,' smiled Barney.

'Outward Bound!' I shouted across the clearing.

We turned and headed back to the tent.

The Day of Reckoning

Jenks cheered Eleanor up good and proper. First off, he gave her his address so she could write to his little sister Brenda.

Brenda had lost touch with Noleen, her American pen-friend, when the Newtsons had moved to Alaska and Splodge had eaten the letter containing the new address. Jenks reckoned she and Eleanor would get on like a house on fire writing about ponies and pop-stars and swapping whinges about their deranged families.

Then he told her about the time his dad accidentally glued himself to the bathroom ceiling while putting up the new tiles and had to be cut down by the fire brigade.

She was beginning to chuckle by now. So he decided to break all the Agent Z confidentiality rules, and explained how we'd wired the bunch of kippers to our history teacher's car engine last term. By this time she was wiping the tears from her eyes.

The two of them were walking back up to the camp when they stumbled across the assorted rabbit-pieces lying scattered in the grass. Jenks picked up the head, poked his fingers inside it, wiggled the mouth and said, 'Gissa a gottle of geer! Gissa a gottle of geer!' And it was at this point that Eleanor had her brainwave.

Barney was unsure whether the plan was possible at first. But he unearthed a needle and thread from the Useful Things box at the bottom of Roz's rucksack and handed them to Eleanor. She took a deep breath and got stuck in.

An hour later, Fforbes-Giraffe and Captain Prat were woken by an eerie were-voice growling, 'I have come for revenge. I am the rabbit-ghoul of Llanpwllgogwych. May the curse be upon you. You will find yourselves on the toilet . . . forever!'

They came round, rubbed their eyes and saw, hovering over them, the disembodied head of their dinner, moving its mouth in a way that would have made a Hollywood special effects studio jealous. It took them a second or two to discover the length of cotton disappearing up through a neatly scissored hole in the top of their tent, but a second or two of garbled screaming was entertainment enough.

We got all the nasty jobs next day, of course: cleaning away the fire, filling in the overused latrine, chipping off the fossilized porridge Penny had somehow fused into the metal of the cooking pan. They just assumed it was us. Eleanor was a total weed. Potato-Head was a grown-up. Penny wouldn't have risked getting gizzard all over her nail-varnish. And Roz couldn't have done an eerie were-growl without having a serious medical problem.

We couldn't care less. Tonight was the big night. When you're running a fifty-fifty chance of being in a coffin before breakfast, toilet-duties pale into insignificance.

Barney knew I was on for it, if only because I didn't want him to risk death in a hale of bullets all on his own. I couldn't stomach the thought of looking across at his empty desk in Geography every Monday morning and thinking how I'd chickened out.

Jenks, on the other hand, held firm. Barney plugged away at him all morning, but to no effect whatsoever.

'OK,' Barney sighed, eventually, as we followed Penny and Fforbes-Giraffe down through a copse of pine trees. 'You just stay in your tent, tucked up in your little sleeping bag counting sheep while Ben and I go out and battle against the forces of evil.'

'You don't get it, do you,' Jenks insisted. 'If you end up dead, or in hospital, or in prison, or all mashed up at the bottom of some cliff, they'll be after my guts.'

'Who will?' I asked.

'Grenade-Head. And his mates.' Jenks was hotching from one foot to the other, as if the ground had got too hot for him. 'And the police. And Potato-Head. And Lanchester. And Breezeblock. And your parents. And they'll all be saying, "Why didn't you do anything, Jenkinson? Why did you let your stupid friends go off like that? Why didn't you tell somebody? It's all your fault."' He stopped and stared hard at Barney, his eyes going all glassy and narrow, like the fire-chief in *Brain-Worms* after they've crawled down his ear-hole and eaten away the inside of his head. 'I'm not going to let you do it.'

'And how are you going to do that?' asked Barney, folding his arms and waiting.

Jenks shoved his lower lip out and seemed stumped for a second or two. Then the bulb clicked on above his head and he gave us a smirky, self-satisfied little grin.

'Like this,' he announced.

He turned, took five paces along the muddy path then veered sideways and strode, face-first, into a large pine-tree.

'Aaaaargh!' he screamed, stumbling backwards.

'You'll have to try harder than that,' said Barney. 'Break your leg, at least.'

But Jenks was staggering back and forth through the undergrowth with his arms stretched out in front of him, wailing, 'Help! Help! I can't see! I'm blind! Everything's gone black! Help! Get me to a doctor!'

I had to admit, Jenks put on a good show. It took a minute or so for everyone to run back to where we were standing, and another minute before Potato-Head was himself running round in circles gibbering, 'Oh my God! What are we going to do? How did this happen? Oh my God! Someone get hold of him. Wait. No. Calm down.

We have to think clearly. Oh my God!'

Captain Prat took command. The map was unfolded and Roz was given directions to the nearest road. She would flag down a car and catch a lift to a phonebox. Meanwhile, the rest of us were to start carrying Jenks directly down the hill.

'Hang on a moment,' said Barney, stepping through the crowd, 'I think I might be able to save everyone a lot of time and energy.'

'Aaargh! I'm blind! Help me!' Jenks whined, overdoing it a bit by this time.

'That's very kind of you,' said Potato-Head. 'But Jenkinson really needs to see a doctor, and as fast as possible.'

'If you could all stand back, please.' Barney strode into the undergrowth and returned carrying a huge log covered with a gruesome assortment of knobbles and spikes.

'What on earth do you think you're . . . ?' asked Potato-Head.

But sheer horror made him speechless. Barney waited for Jenks to stumble towards him, his eyes staring blankly ahead. Then he silently lifted the fearsome weapon high in the air. He paused to make sure Jenks had seen what he was doing, then heaved it downwards towards the top of Jenks' head.

Poor Jenks. He'd tried hard. But he wasn't going to try that hard. The knobbled log was only centimetres from his scalp when he finally gave in and leapt backwards to avoid being puréed. The log-end buried itself in the forest floor with a satisfying 'Donk!'.

Potato-Head was still trembling when Barney patted him on the back, said, 'See? Miracle cure. Works every time,' and headed off up the path.

Jenks got a second chance whilst we were pitching camp.

'Hey, boys. Got a proposition for you,' said Roz, wandering over and squatting on my rucksack.

'Uh-huh?' I said, scraping the crispy packet-soup stain off our groundsheet.

Barney sniffed the inside of his sleeping bag, turned it inside out and hung it over a branch to air. 'Try us.'

'Just been up on the ridge over there. The Yellows are camping a couple of miles away at the bottom of the next hill.' She flicked out the biggest blade of her pen-knife and began excavating the dirt from under her fingernails. 'What do you say we wait till bedtime then sneak over and cause a bit of havoc, eh? Glue up a few tent-zips so they can't get out. Saw half-way through their latrine-seat. Rig up some trip-wires. You know the sort of thing.'

'Sounds cool,' mused Barney. 'But . . .'

'Not tonight,' I added.

'Hey!' she complained. 'What's up with you? You're boys, aren't you? Boys are meant to spend their time playing football and smashing windows and setting off stink bombs. Trashing the Yellows should be right up your alley. Go on. Show me some macho.'

'Honestly, Roz. I didn't expect you to be so old-fashioned,' said Barney, polishing the base of the porridge pan and holding it up to check his hairstyle. 'Wake up. This is the nineteen-nineties. We're New Men.' I nodded in agreement, wondering what on earth he was on about. 'Tell you what . . . Let's be really right-on. You go and find Eleanor Beasley. Then the two of you can get your knees all scabby crawling down to the Yellow camp and giving them gyp. And while you're doing that, Ben, Jenks and I can hang around here in the warm, drinking tea and chatting about babies and shopping. Sound groovy?'

Jenks gave Barney a puzzled, angry look, then turned to Roz. 'Don't listen to him. He's a wally.' He stood up. 'I'll come. I'll help you.'

'Sorry, Jenks. Need a team for this one.' She picked up a stick and began whittling it.

'You and me. We can be a team,' Jenks insisted.

'Forget it,' she said flatly.

Jenks stared glumly at his shoes. He pursed his lips and you could see the steam start to leak out of his ears. When he finally spoke, he sounded like a four-year-old whose plastic tricycle has been taken away. 'I'll tell you why they won't go with you. I'll tell you what they're actually doing tonight . . .'

The palm of Barney's hand smacked his mouth shut with an audible pop.

'Hey, come on, Jenks, mate. Don't spoil it,' said Barney. 'This is meant to be a really nice surprise for everyone. Just because I wouldn't let you use my Mickey Mouse toothbrush, there's no need to get all huffy.'

Somehow, Barney managed to sound relaxed and grandfatherly while keeping Jenks' face in a python-grip and wrestling him to the ground.

'Nnnn! Gk! Rbrbp!' grunted Jenks.

'Shut it!' whispered Barney, now seated firmly in the middle of Jenks' chest. 'Or I'll brain you. Permanently. Understand?'

Roz stood up. 'You haven't really got the hang of this New Man thing, have you?' She looked at Jenks as he struggled to breathe under Barney's weight, and shook her head sadly. 'Perhaps you lot aren't the best bet for a job like this after all.' She turned and walked away into the darkness. 'Enjoy talking about babies.'

Jenks got his third chance just after eleven. And this time he made no mistakes.

'Check balaclavas, Z-Two,' said Barney.

'Yeh,' I said, handing him one and putting mine on. 'Got 'em.'

'Check flares.'

'Yep.'

Barney let his arms flop to his side and stared at me. 'Ben. You have to get into this.'

'OK, OK,' I grumped.

'Right.' He gave me the balaclava back. 'Let's start again.'

I closed my eyes, took a deep breath and forced myself into the mood.

I cast my mind back to the training course we'd done in the Brecon Beacons with the SAS last month. Strictly speaking, they needed six months to knock us into shape, so Major Grizedale said. But we didn't have the time to spare. By then, Morrison would be sunning himself in South America. We had to be transformed into steel-nerved fighting machines inside four weeks.

They made the course as tough as they could. So tough that Heckleston ended up in hospital. So tough that Chivers is still receiving counselling to stop him crying all the time.

'Let 'em go,' spat Grizedale. 'We don't need wimps.'

We learnt how to pluck a hedgehog and eat it raw. We learnt the two-fingers-in-the-eye-socket defence against leaping attack dogs. We learnt how to take

bullets out of our own legs with a sharpened stick, tourniquet the wound and then do an assault course. We learnt jujitsu and karate. We learnt how to jump through the windscreen of a moving Land-Rover and knock the driver unconscious with a micro-jab to the pressure-point under his ear.

We were as ready as we were ever going to be.

'OK, Z-One,' I said. 'Let's load up.'

'Yo,' replied Barney. 'Check balaclavas.'

'Balaclavas, check.' I handed one back to Barney.

'Check flares, Z-Two.'

'Flares, check.'

'Check matches . . .'

We slipped out of the tenthole into the night. The fire was nothing more than embers now. And the moon was hidden above thick, obscuring cloud. It was perfect. We slipped across the clearing like black ghosts.

Unexpectedly, the silence was broken by a bustle of feathers from the nearby foliage. We froze. A tawny owl took wing and swooped through the camp, banking between our two unmoving heads. The training had worked. It didn't even know we were there. We were invisible.

And silent, too. We moved onward, placing our hypersensitive toes effortlessly between the crackly twigs onto the spongey earth.

'See you later, lads,' said a loud voice. It was Jenks, emerging from the tent behind us. 'Have fun. I'm just popping down the latrine.'

We waited for him to disappear down the slope, then slipped into the shadows.

'Stage Two,' said Barney. 'No talking from now until the mission is complete. And remember the Agent Z Code. Each of us is on our own from here on in. If one of us falls into enemy hands, the other has to get the information back to base. This is no time for sentiment or friendship. This thing is worth more than either of us. We're expendable, kid. If you want to back out, back out now.'

'I'm with you all the way, Captain.'

'Alrighty.' He flipped up the lid of his luminous compass. '34 degrees South-West. Let's hit the road.'

We were just entering the undergrowth at the perimeter of the camp, when I heard a faint voice behind me. Turning I saw Jenks, at the foot of the hill, standing outside Potato-Head's tent, knocking limply on the canvas, and saying, 'Sir . . . ? Sir . . . ?'

I turned towards Barney and opened my mouth. Then I shut it again. No noise. This was Stage Two. Let Jenkinson squeal. We always knew he was the weak link in the chain. So, he was going to blow the whole thing wide open. It didn't matter now. He'd left it too late by a long chalk. We'd be there first. When the cavalry arrived at St Dominic's, there'd be nothing left to do but mop up. We'd be long gone by then.

I turned and melted into the darkness.

Fireworks

I knew I'd be wetting myself. But I thought I'd be wetting myself about Grenade-Head and Nosher and Sugs and the sawn-off, pump-action shotguns. As it was, I hardly thought about them. It was the dark I was wetting myself about.

It's stupid. It's like getting shoved off a forty-storey building and noticing, halfway down, that there's a tarantula going up your trouser leg. It doesn't matter, of course. In two seconds you're going to be a stain on the roof of a phone box. But you still panic. It's natural.

You see, I'd never found myself smack in the middle of one hundred per cent, no-holds-barred darkness before. My bedroom is opposite the Seven-Eleven and spitting distance from the dual carriageway. You can draw the curtains, but you can still see the belisha beacons going on and off through the Flintstones pattern. You can shut yourself in the airing cupboard, but there's still a sliver of landing-light illuminating Dad's Y-fronts.

Nothing had prepared me for three hundred square miles of darkness as black as the inside of a lump of coal.

We were making our way towards a bunch of toughs who'd fill us full of lead if they so much as spotted us. But all that I could think about were the hoards of noiseless, fanged Ted Hughes psycho-killer beasties slithering towards me out of the night.

I remembered a picture book I read when I was six. *Jumpy Jimmy and the Bogger with Big Teeth*. In the book, Jimmy refuses to go to sleep because he's sure there's a bogger hiding under the bed just waiting to wolf him down. Mum tells him to wise up and get some shut-eye, then shoves off downstairs to watch *Match of The Day* and fix herself a whisky, or whatever she gets up to when she's not in the book. And Jimmy is trying to go to sleep when the whole bed starts to shake. It's the bogger, of course. But he's cute and cuddly and he and Jimmy spend the night dancing around together in that daft way that kids and monsters do in picture books.

The story was meant to make kids like the dark, so they'd be snoring as soon as their heads hit the pillow and their parents didn't have to video *Match of the Day*.

Not me. It scared me witless. Like Mum says, I've got an artistic imagination. For six months I refused to get into bed without shining a torch underneath it and

poking about with a pointy bamboo cane from the shed in case the bogger was invisible.

Now the bogger had returned.

And he'd grown up, on account of all those sci-fi films I'd watched in the interim. Bogger Mk II had infra-red night-vision goggles and a carbon-fibre, rolly frog-tongue with a poisoned velcro end-piece that could take a tawny owl out of the air at a hundred metres.

So, when Barney screamed, I thought he'd been eaten.

He hadn't. Three seconds later, I heard him say, irritatedly, 'Ben? Ben? Where are you? Come and help me, you wazzock.'

I sidled through the pokey twigs, bumped into Barney

and lit a match. His face was a mess. He had just head-butted a squashy, orange tree-fungus.

'Pretty scarey, eh?' he whispered.

He had the willies good and proper, I could tell. I was relieved. If Barney was bricking it, bricking it was normal.

'Maintain silence, Z-One,' I hissed. 'This is Stage Two. Give me a direction reading.'

'Oh . . . er . . . right . . . Of course,' he said, fiddling with the compass.

I felt deliciously superior.

'On target,' he said. 'Half a mile or so still to go.'

'Carry on,' I replied brusquely and headed onward into the dark.

We knew we had arrived when we heard the waterfall: a dull, churning roar which seemed to come out of the ground itself. We homed in.

Only when we reached the clearing that surrounded the monastery and peered out of the overhanging foliage, did we realize that the cloud had thinned. There was a perfect semicircle of moon suspended above the far trees. The fallen stones and jagged walls were drenched in a cold, blue light. High above the ruin, it was just possible to make out the last remaining arch, a thin, silhouetted hoop blocking out the stars.

Silently, we laid ourselves down in the thick brambles. Barney passed me the three flares and the matches. I arranged them in front of me. He took out the camera from his jacket pocket and ran a check on it, shielding the green LED readout with his hand. We looked backwards into the trees and memorized the direction back towards the camp. When they arrived, we'd be pinned down. And when the flares went off, we'd have one chance and one chance only. We'd have to take the photograph and move like whippets.

We waited.

Barney checked his watch. 11:56.

We waited some more.

12:00. 12:05. 12:10.

I grew nervous. Perhaps they were casing the area, sweeping through the undergrowth in a long arc to check for police before moving in.

We carried on waiting.

Gradually, my nervousness began to fade away. We'd got it all wrong. We must have done. They were meeting outside the St Dominic's Cinema in Bangor. The morse was just a waggly torch belonging to some berk camping across the lake. The newspaper photo was of Grenade-Head's delinquent cousin. Whatever. It didn't matter. What mattered was that there was no rendezvous. We were going to walk back to the camp and I was going to have the best night's sleep I'd had in my life.

What the hell, maybe we'd even take a detour via the Yellow camp and rig up a tripwire or two.

Then I heard the voice.

'. . . I'll meet up with you at Beddgelert, on the Aberglaslyn Road . . . No way . . . No monkey business . . . That's fine by me . . .'

It was Grenade-Head. No mistake. He was inside the

monastery, only metres away from us. He must have been there all the time.

I felt every hair on my head winch itself upright. I breathed slowly and deeply, like Chrissy Tucker did on *Wallaby Springs* when she was in labour with Lonny, and the flying doctor came over the radio to say they were having to turn back because of electrical storms over the desert, but they should get out lots of clean towels and hot water and he'd talk them through the whole thing.

'. . . Make up your mind . . .' Grenade-Head's voice rang out again, then fell silent.

Barney's hand pressed down hard on my shoulder. 'Easy!' he whispered.

He was right. I was twitching. Thorns were scratching my ankles, there was a twig up my nose and my hands were shaking. My legs badly wanted to run.

Time ticked by, like it does during that bit in the films where the hero falls unconscious at the wheel and the car keeps accelerating down the mountain road towards the hairpin bend over the crevasse.

'Let's move in,' whispered Barney, gripping my shirt and pulling me to my feet.

Move in? Was he crazy? Why didn't we just stand up and shout, 'Hey! We're over here! Come and kill us!'

I clung to the grass.

'We're never going to see anything from here,' he insisted, letting go of me and crawling out of the shadows. 'We're not coming all this way for nothing.'

I watched his fat body snake through the moonlit grass

in front of me. He looked like a boa constrictor that has had a whole sheep for lunch. And the further he went, the lonelier I felt. I needed that big, bullet-deflecting body next to mine.

I gathered the flares, dragged a bough of scratchy brambles over my head and headed after him, arms out, bum down, the blood drumming in my ears.

We covered twenty metres of open ground and folded ourselves into the shadows of the nearest friary wall. I looked back. If they found us now, they'd have ten seconds to take aim before we hit the trees. My only hope would be to zig-zag better than Barney did.

'Get the flares ready,' hissed Barney, turning and shimmying towards the break in the wall.

I took out three flares, opened the match-box, quivered, spilt the contents of the box on the grass, fumbled for the matches, picked up a handful, dropped the box, lost it, fumbled . . .

'Empty,' whispered Barney, re-shimmying back towards me. 'Take a butcher's.'

His fist hoiked me along the wall to the opening. I peered round into the ruined building. Grass. Boulders. Shadows. Nothing.

No. Not quite. In the middle of the long, grass rectangle sat a small, black object the size of a fat dictionary.

'Look,' I whispered. 'There.'

His finger waggled in front of my face beckoning me to follow. He hoisted himself over the crumbled stones and made his way towards the centre of the ruin, crouching and swivelling at each step to scan the surrounding darkness. I tip-toed behind him. My heart sounded like a V-8 Land-Rover engine turning over.

We were halfway towards the black object when we heard the voice again.

'. . . I run a tight ship here . . .'

I span. And span back again. The voice was painfully clear. He was only metres away. But where? Barney grabbed me and began sprint-creeping back towards the gap in the wall.

A branch broke somewhere outside the ruin. On the other side of the gap. We halted. Footsteps on grass. Another click. Harder this time. A safety catch? A shot-gun cartridge being pushed home?

I forced my wobbling legs to retrace their steps, dragging Barney in front of me for protection. Slowly we retreated towards the thick shadows at the far end of the room. I heard the tiny, oiled snick of Barney unfolding his penknife. I could almost feel the bullet-holes peppering my waterproof. I imagined Mr Lanchester breaking the sad news to Mum.

A silhouetted figure appeared in the gap.

Max Bygraves was a complete surprise.

There was sudden blast of keyboard music and I heard, from somewhere near my right ankle, 'I'm dreaming of a white Christmas . . . with every Christmas card I write . . .'

I screamed.

Then the rockets went off. There was a short, fierce fizz, a flash of brilliant tangerine light, and the two aerial torpedoes screamed towards us, streaked over our heads and hit the far wall. By then the Catherine wheel and the Roman candle were alight.

I stopped screaming. I didn't have the spare breath. I was running round in a circle flapping my arms in the air. I knew I was going to die. And soon. It seemed like the thing you were meant to do.

What I shouldn't have done was to throw the flares away, in an enclosed space, what with all those Catherine wheel sparks flying all over the place and everything. But the Firework Code wasn't uppermost in my mind at the time.

'. . . where snowflakes glisten . . . and children listen . . . to sleigh-bells tinkling in the snow . . .'

'FSSSSSSSSSHH!' hissed the flares.

'Run!' screamed Barney as the flaming, pink torches started to ricochet and somersault around the walls.

I had forgotten the silhouetted figure standing at the doorway until I ran into it. I felt a fleshy whack across my face and chest, and stumbled backwards into Barney.

A flare flipped towards us and Roz's face was illuminated in shocking pink.

'. . . dreaming of a white Christmas . . .'

She stepped round us and walked towards the centre of the ruin. 'Damn,' she huffed. 'Borrowed the tape off Mum. Should've remembered to record over it right to the end.' Bending down, she pressed a button on what I could now see was a portable tape-recorder.

'. . . just like the ones we used to Ker-chunk!'

'Wha . . . ?' Barney was looking around idiotically,

like a cartoon cat just after the ten-ton weight has smacked it on the head.

'Congratulations,' smiled Roz, walking back towards us. She took a family-sized, gold-paper-wrapped chocolate bar out of her back pocket, broke it in half and handed it to us. 'Have some GettyBank bullion, boys.'

My hand rose of its own accord and took hold of the bar. I'd have eaten her shoe if she'd offered it to me. My brain was putty.

She disappeared momentarily through the gap in the wall, then reappeared carrying a small paraffin lamp and a folded camping stool. She struck a match, lit the lamp, unfolded the stool and sat herself down.

'Got to hand it to you, lads. Honestly didn't believe I'd ever find anyone stupid enough to fall for this scam. But I really hit the jackpot with you lot, didn't I. Hook, line and sinker. You were fabulous.' She began to laugh. 'Look, if you're not going to eat any of that chocolate, at least give me some, I'm starving.'

She retrieved the half-bar still dangling on the end of my outstretched arm.

'Stupid?' I spluttered. 'Stupid?'

'Hang on . . .' Barney put his hands on either side of his head, as if he was trying to stop it bursting. 'Look . . . I mean . . .'

'The newspaper clipping?' she suggested, breaking off a chunk of chocolate and putting it into her mouth.

'Yeh,' replied Barney. 'The newspaper clipping. Just for starters.'

'Good, wasn't it,' she said, taking her time, so that she

could really appreciate our flabbergastedness. 'One of my photographs of Ed from four years ago, when he had a beard. Got a xerox done at the local copy-shop, had it reduced, stuck it on an old newspaper article and photocopied the whole thing. Crafty, eh?'

'Four years ago?' I asked, flummoxed.

'Yeh. Come here every summer for a holiday.'

'And scare the living daylights out of people?' I was trying to sound cool and laid back, but I couldn't do it. I was still shaking. I sounded like Jenks' little sister, Brenda, did when he took the brakes off her bike, or climbed in through her bedroom window wearing his day-glo vampire-mask.

'Yeh. Sometimes.' Roz smiled patiently at me. 'Got my older brother to ring up last year and say there'd been a massive leak at the Trawsfynydd nuclear power station. Had everyone hiding in the cellar for an afternoon trying to seal the door with butter from the store to keep the radioactive gas out. That sort of thing. But nothing like this. Not for lack of trying, mind. Been lugging that briefcase down from Doncaster every year, and priming kids about the little door next to the girls' washroom. But no-one had your spectacular gullibility, I'm afraid to say.'

Barney was still holding his head. 'The morse . . .'

'Paddled across the lake with a torch.'

'*Heartbreak Hotel?*'

'Your friend Winston. Paid him three Flakes. Wanted him to do the opening bars of *Beethoven's Fifth*, but he said you weren't cultured enough to recognize it. He said Elvis Presley would ring a bell.'

I wanted to relax and have a good laugh about all this. But it was like stubbing your toe. All that angriness just goes wooshing round and round inside you until you get it out by swearing or hitting something.

'You don't realize, do you?' I spat. 'You don't realize what we went through. I thought I was going to be killed. I could have been expelled from school. I ended up dangling from a rope only inches above Dawson's head outside him and Lanchester's room in the middle of the night . . .'

Roz began chuckling. No wonder. It had seemed like the end of the world at the time. It sounded ludicrous now.

'Looks like you had a grand old time,' she said. 'Incidentally, chaps, I'd take those balaclavas off, if I were you. You look like a couple of right berks at the moment.'

Barney slipped his off as suavely as he could, bit into his chocolate then reached out to shake Roz's hand. 'My compliments,' he said. 'You had us over a barrel.'

'Jenks,' I said quietly, catching Barney's eye. 'Jenks. I didn't tell you. I saw him going to Potato-Head's tent just as we were leaving.'

'So?' Barney shrugged and munched.

'He was going to tell him everything. It's the only explanation.' I turned to Roz. 'He thought we were all going to die, too. He *still* thinks we're all going to die.'

'Chill out,' said Barney. 'Potato-Head'll just tell him to calm down and go back to sleep. Think about it, Ben.

What would you say if Jenks came and told you his mates were tracking down a gang of armed bank raiders, eh?' He patted my knee. 'It hurts me to say this, Ben, mate, but even Potato-Head isn't as stupid as we are.'

'Suppose so,' I muttered.

And, as if by magic, it was at precisely this moment that Jenks loomed out of the darkness, doing his headless chicken routine, scampering back and forth saying, 'What the . . . ? Where are . . . ? What happened . . . ?

'Talk of the devil,' said Roz.

'Look out!' shouted Barney. 'He's behind you!'

Jenks twizzled round, ducking and covering his head to protect himself from the gunfire. And, Barney was right, there was someone behind him. But it wasn't Nosher. Or Sugs. It was Potato-Head.

He strode into the light and said, 'Would someone like to tell me what on earth is happening?' He was wearing the clumpy brown glasses he used when his contact lenses were soaking. And you could see the bottoms of his paisley-patterned pyjamas poking out from beneath his track-suit trousers.

'It's a long story,' said Barney, 'and you probably wouldn't believe us anyway.'

'You!' he stammered. 'Your legs!'

'What about my legs?' asked, Barney, checking them.

'You're meant to have multiple fractures.' He turned towards Jenks and glowered.

Jenks hotched and smiled pathetically 'I couldn't tell him the truth, could I? He wouldn't have believed me. And I had to get help. I *had* to.'

'The truth?' Potato-Head fumed. 'And what is the truth?' He breathed deeply, preparing himself for a new, and even more grotesque, disaster. 'You've killed someone? You've burnt something down?' He paused, checked our sheepish faces and let himself relax a little. 'My God, this explanation had better be good.'

Jenks still hadn't twigged. 'No. No. It's really serious,' he insisted. 'Grenade-Head . . . I mean, Ed Michaels. He's a bank robber. His real name's Harry Morrison. He escaped from Dartmoor. He shot three security guards and he's meeting up with the other blokes who didn't get caught. Here. Tonight. And they've got all this gold bullion stashed some . . .'

He ground slowly to a halt. He had finally noticed Roz, and realized that she was meant to be sawing through latrine seats over in the next valley. Somewhere deep inside his brain, the vital connection had been made.

'Ah . . .' he said.

Barney and I put our heads in our hands and winced. Potato-Head's jaw swung open like a castle drawbridge.

'Have you gone completely off your trolley?' he asked Jenks.

'Never on it in the first place,' said Barney, to himself.

'Look,' said Roz, 'I think there's been a bit of misunderstanding . . .'

'Wait. Wait,' said Potato-Head. This was all going too fast for him. He held up his hand to slow things down. 'First things first . . . No-one's been hurt, right?'

'Nope,' I reassured him

He let out a long, whistly sigh and rubbed his eyes. 'Thank God for that.'

'Sorry, Sir,' said Barney. 'Have some chocolate.'

Potato-Head shook his head, broke off a choc-chunk, muttered, 'Lord preserve us,' popped the chunk into his mouth and chomped. Then he stopped chomping. He looked like someone who has just remembered leaving their grandmother sitting on a busy train line. He whapped his forehead and swore, ejecting a splotch of dribbly chocolate onto my trousers.

'Sir?' I said.

'No, no, no, no, no!' he groaned, clutching his face in his hands. 'I've just remembered. I got the mountain rescue team out. I told them there was a kid with a smashed-up leg out here on the mountain . . .' He had gone sheet-white.

'How?' I asked. 'How did you call them out?'

'With carrier pigeons, Ben,' he said sarcastically, pulling a walkie-talkie from his back pocket and holding it like you might hold a pinless grenade. 'They don't let us take a pack of raving whackoes like you lot out into the wilderness without some way of getting hold of help fast.'

'Sneaky,' said Barney. 'You kept that one quiet.'

But Potato-Head was turning and staring out into the darkness. 'They're going to be here any minute. I'm going to be done for.' He leant against the nearest wall and began slowly banging his head against the moss-covered stonework. 'Why does it always happen to me, eh? What have I done wrong? First, that damned dog running across the road in front of that ice-cream van. Now this. Breezeblock is going to have me for breakfast. I can see it now. Goodbye promotion. Goodbye references. Goodbye teaching. Two weeks from now and I'm going to be stacking shelves in Sainsbury's, all because of you lot.'

'Relax,' said Barney. 'It'll be fine. We'll just do some heavy sucking-up. We'll say we're really sorry. It just happened that a few wires got crossed here and there. And, well . . .' He pinched his lips and waited momentarily for the idea to brew. 'I know . . . We were having this dry-run. Emergency rescue skills and all that. You know, stretcher-making, tourniquets, the biz. And you got the wrong end of the stick and thought it was real and did what any sane, sensible, upright citizen would do . . .'

Potato-Head wasn't listening. He was having a brainwave of his own. 'No,' he spluttered. 'No. It'll be alright. I remember now. I didn't give my name. They don't know who made the call. I could've been Bob. I could've been any of the staff. Even . . . Yes, maybe even one of you lot.' He was getting excited now. 'Maybe, say, one of you kids nicked the walkie-talkie. Yes. That's right.'

With no warning, he stepped back from the wall, took the walkie-talkie from his back pocket again, executed a neat discus-swivel and hurled the gizmo far into the night sky.

There was a faint clattering of snapped branches, then a stunned silence. And it was in the stunned silence that we heard them. Distant voices. Big boots. The panting of a dog. A beam of torchlight swinging back and forth somewhere deep inside the tangled trees.

'The mountain rescue team,' squeaked Potato-Head. 'They're coming!' He lunged towards Roz's paraffin lamp and wrestled with it until it went out. 'Move! Come on! Move! They mustn't see us. If we're still here when they arrive we're done for.'

'*You're* done for, you mean,' said Barney coolly, squatting unmoved on his up-ended stone and idly selecting his next piece of chocolate.

Potato-Head stood in front of him, bent down, pressed his nose against Barney's nose and hissed, with impressive venom, 'How would you like to find yourself in detention every week from now until doomsday, Smart-Alec? This is my job we're talking about here. So, shift. Now.'

'OK. OK. I give in,' said Barney, standing and brushing the chocolate crumbs from his track-suit trousers. 'You're a hard man, Mr Dawson.'

'Shut up and run!' hissed Potato-Head.

We stuffed our assorted gubbins into Roz's rucksack, slung it over Jenks' shoulder and high-tailed it into the night.

Aaaaiieeeeeh!

It all turned out rather well in the end.

Not for Jenks, it has to be admitted. He ended up breaking his leg. And breaking your leg is not fun at the best of times. Though it did mean that the next time he wheeled out his Gory-Mountaineering-Injuries routine, he was able to illustrate it with stomach-churning details drawn from his own personal experience.

On the plus side, Potato-Head's frantic walkie-talkie call turned out to be justified after all. And as for the rest of us, we got a chance to practise our Outward Bound emergency skills in a Real Life Situation. A truly thrilling and value-for-money climax to the entire fortnight, in fact.

It was Jenks' Olympic qualifying sprint-performance

which was his downfall. That, and his eagerness to get away from trouble as fast as humanly possible.

It could have been a whole lot worse, of course. If he hadn't screamed so helpfully, we would all have gone over the edge along with him, lemming-style. You see, it hadn't occurred to us that when a mountain river plunges fifty metres in a spectacular waterfall, it's because the ground has plunged fifty metres underneath it. But we were running at the time, not thinking. And it was so dark, under the trees, we might as well have been wearing duffel bags on our heads.

'What the flaming heck was that . . . ?' shouted Potato-Head as Jenks' shriek rose above the roar of the water, faded ominously, then disappeared.

It sounded like a flak-riddled spitfire heading for a total wipe-out in *The Battle of Britain*.

'Jenks!' I yelped, accelerating.

'Whoa!' bellowed Barney, yanking my trouser-belt backwards. 'Careful!'

'Oh no! Oh no! Oh no!' Potato-Head began wailing at the sky.

We dropped onto all fours and crawled nervously towards the edge of the precipice. Roz excavated the torch from Barney's pocket and swung the cone of light back and forth in the darkness below.

Water. Foam. Rock. More water. Then, ten metres below us, a scrawny tree jutting from the rocky wall. And in the middle of the scrawny tree, Jenks, his legs knotted into its branches in a way which did not seem biologically possible.

The rucksack was dangling from his waist, its contents falling, one by one, into the river: paraffin lamp, balaclava, camping stool, balaclava . . . Above the sound of the water, I could just hear Max Bygraves singing, '. . . with every Christmas card I write . . .'

'Gordon Bennet . . . !' I put my hand over my mouth and looked away.

When I looked back, Jenks had recovered from the shock and started to scream again. The sound was dulled by the noise of the thrashing water, but you could have fitted a football into his mouth. I hadn't seen someone scream like that since Mrs Ebsworth watched the power-saw come out of Cyril's lunch-box in *Blood Frenzy*.

'Shirts. Jackets,' ordered Roz. 'Get them off and knot them together. Make a rope. And give me a belt to tie round his shoulders so we can lift him. I'm going down.'

'No!' shouted Potato-Head. 'I mean yes. I mean I'll go down.' He struggled out of his jacket to reveal an over-tight pyjama-top and an acre of hairy, doormat belly.

I whipped off my track-suit trousers and knotted them between the jacket and Barney's shirt. Roz and Potato-Head inched their legs into the darkness below the overhang. Barney unbuckled his trouser belt and handed it down.

It was all the fault of those stupid shelves Mrs Dawson had insisted that he put up in the back bathroom two years ago, so Potato-Head explained later. She already had enough shelves to house the contents of The British

Library, but he wasn't one to argue with a full-blown psychopathic obsession, so he toddled down to the builder's merchants on Saturday morning after breakfast.

He should have put his foot down right at the beginning. If he hadn't given in, he wouldn't have found himself flapping around on the top of that antique step-ladder he borrowed from Clive Winkleton next door. If he'd had a proper ladder he wouldn't have backflipped onto the side of the bath and slipped that disc. And if his back wasn't quite so dodgy he might have been able to haul that idiot Jenkinson back up that infernal cliff-face without his old injury flaring up and rendering him totally immobile.

'Aaarghk!' gasped Potato-Head, his slipped-disc going into spasm.

'Ben, we need some help down here!' shouted Roz.

'Are you alright, Sir?' I hollered.

'The walkie-talkie!' he was yelling to himself. 'I threw the walkie-talkie away! I threw the walkie-talkie away!'

He seemed to have gone irreversibly bananas.

'The flares, Barney,' I said. 'Light a flare. The mountain rescue team can't be too far away. And you can see a flare for miles. Quick.'

'Good thinking, Batman.' He dug into my little shoulder-bag. There was one flare left.

And no matches.

'Belly-button fluff,' said Barney. 'That's it. I'll get some dry tinder and stones.' He disappeared off into the darkness leaving me holding the slowly lengthening arm of Potato-Head's jacket.

By the time he returned, Potato-Head was shouting, 'Your pyjamas. They're disintegrating!'

Barney emptied his belly-button, rolled me over to ferret around in mine, added a handful of fluff-balls from the arm of Potato-Head's jacket, bunched them up with the tinder and began whacking stones.

'What the hell are you doing up there?' shouted Potato-Head.

'Yo!' cheered Barney. 'We have ignition!'

He stuffed the flare's blue touch-paper into the tiny flame, let it catch, stood up, wound his arm back and hurled the thing high into the air.

The world went pink. The flare soared up and up and up, then banked, corkscrewed, and began rocketing downwards. I screamed. Barney did a body swerve, the flare hit the grass, bounced, singed a hole in his jeans, flipped over the edge of the ravine and screamed down into the water, very nearly adding a heart-attack to Potato-Head's rapidly growing list of medical problems.

The paramedics, Dave and Tony, were very pleasant about the whole thing. Sure, they'd been dragged out of nice, warm beds. But that was the whole point of the job, wasn't it.

And Jenks had only broken his leg, that was all. The syringeful of anaesthetic they'd pumped into his arm would keep him happy till he reached the Porthmadog casualty unit. They saw much worse all the time. Jenks' leg was still attached to the rest of his body, for one thing. Which was more than you could say for some of the people they scraped off the mountain.

OK, ordering the helicopter out was maybe a touch over the top, but the man who made the call just before midnight had described some truly horrific injuries. Never mind. People often got over-excited when these sort of accidents happened. But that didn't matter. Better to come looking for someone with no head and find a few grazed knees rather than find someone with no head when all you'd brought were sticking plasters and antiseptic cream.

'Ooh, look!' babbled Jenks, grinning from ear to ear, as the air above us was flooded with the glare of the helicopter's searchlights and the whackity-whack of rotor blades. 'Iss a big, lellow kelly-hopter! Lellow-kopter! Jelly, wello, big-big chopter-kopter!'

He seemed to be coping with the pain very well indeed.

'Have you got a spare syringe-ful of that stuff?' asked Potato-Head as he lay stretched out on the grass.

'A cup of tea is all you need, Sir,' said Dave.

He and Tony finished splinting Jenks' leg and began stretchering him back to the clearing where the chopper had landed. Barney, Roz and I laid Potato-Head out flat on the grass, rolled him onto the second stretcher, heaved him off the ground and followed the two paramedics into the trees.

Strictly speaking, we weren't meant to get a ride in the helicopter. We had a dose of flare-singes, bramble-scratches and precipice bruises between us, that was all. Nothing to justify aerial evacuation. But Flight-Lieutenant 'Dogger' MacKinnon was a bit of a softie at heart. And, besides, as Tony pointed out, since we'd removed most of our warm clothing and hurled it down into the rapids, there was a genuine chance of exposure if we wandered back to the camp half-naked.

'Go on then,' he said. 'Hop in.'

'Mega,' I said.

'Cheers,' said Barney, shaking Dave and Tony's hands in turn.

'Stop dithering and get your bums on board!' yelled Dogger above the roar of the engines.

I hauled Barney in through the hatch, and Dave shunted the door across. 'Chocks away, chaps!' shouted Dogger. The rotors picked up speed and the floor of the helicopter lurched to one side as we lifted clear of the ground.

'Weez is flyingy,' said Jenks.

I looked out of the tiny glass porthole. Way below the fat, black tyres, the falling water flashed and tumbled in the chopper's searchlight. I turned and looked back towards the trees. The tiny figures of Dave and Tony, standing in the middle of the clearing, began to shrink into the blue shadows of the ruined monastery as we climbed slowly towards the stars.

Rudolph the Red-Nosed Reindeer

The helicopter ride was a bit too exciting.

'Dogger' MacKinnon was more than just soft. He was a raving lunatic. I was standing behind him, listening intently as he explained the controls to me, when, without warning, he leapt out of his seat.

'You take over for a tic, Sonny,' he shouted, disappearing from the cockpit. 'Got to go and shake a leg. Too much Ovaltine before bedtime.'

The aircraft rolled forward and began to dive towards the ground. Sick with panic, I leapt into the pilot's seat and heaved on the joystick. No response. The controls weren't working.

I opened my mouth to scream but was interrupted by a pat on the back.

'Relax, Ben,' said Barney, pointing to the co-pilot. 'Dual controls. MacKinnon was winding you up.'

The co-pilot winked at me and pulled the helicopter out of the dive. 'Bit of a wag, our captain,' he explained.

'Jeez . . . !' I slumped.

'Thanks for holding the fort, kid,' said Dogger, returning with a stack of cheese and pickle sandwiches. 'Enjoy that?'

'He loved it,' said Barney.

'Hope you haven't stained the seat,' he said casually, as I moved aside. 'Some kids, they get a bit over-excited when you pull the old dual-control gag. Fancy a sandwich?'

It was a relief to feel the solid tarmac of the casualty car-park under our feet.

Barney, Roz and I reassured the crowd of waiting nurses and doctors that we had only superficial wounds, then accompanied Jenks and Potato-Head into the building on their respective stretchers.

'Oranges and lemons, sang the bells of St Clements . . .' chirruped Jenks happily . . . 'When you are rich, sang the bells of Shoreditch . . .'

'He seems well sedated,' remarked the Sister.

'Watch out he doesn't eat any wineglasses,' said Barney. 'Totally barking. Runs in the family.'

Jenks was wheeled away into curtained cubicle No. 6 to have his leg plastered back into one piece. Potato-Head was winched onto the bed in No. 7. We followed him and filled him in on the rudiments of the Big-Boy

Bullion Heist Rendezvous Fiasco.

Roz was setting the scene for the firework finale when Lanchester and Grenade-Head appeared through the parted curtains.

On account of the long night and the mental strain, it took me a moment or two to remember that Grenade-Head wasn't Harry Morrison, and hadn't mown down three security guards. When I reappeared from beneath the bed, Lanchester was snorting, 'I might have known it was you lot . . .' He stopped short. 'Where are your trousers, young man?' he barked, pointing at me.

Grenade-Head interrupted him. 'Forget the trousers. I want the whole story. And fast. What happened to that boy Jenkinson?'

'Well . . . I . . . It's like . . .' Potato-Head blithered. 'You see . . . It's all a bit hazy, to be frank.'

'Mr Dawson's slipped a disc,' I said, trying to take the heat off.

'Sleepwalking,' said Barney. 'Jenks was sleepwalking.'

'Sleepwalking!?' Lanchester exploded.

'Let the boy explain,' said Grenade-Head firmly.

Lanchester narrowed his eyes and gave us a you-can't-pull-the-wool-over-my-eyes scowl.

Barney took no notice. 'Hasn't done it for years.'

'I'll bet he hasn't,' fumed Mr Lanchester to himself.

'It all started, oh, when he was five or so. Wayne, that's his little brother, he set light to his duvet with the kitchen matches. Wayne's like that. The whole family is, come to think of it.' Grenade-Head tapped his foot impatiently. 'Well, the long and the short of it is, poor old

Jenks was nearly fried alive. Inches from death, they said. Anyway, he couldn't sleep at all for three months. And after that, he sleepwalked every night. Had to put a bolt on his bedroom door. Post Traumatic-Stress-Disorder, apparently. PTSD. Like people have after aircraft crashes and stuff.'

'Get to the point,' muttered Grenade-Head.

'Well, it must have been sitting watching that campfire all evening, or something. Brought it all back, maybe. We woke up and he was gone. When we caught up with him he was half-way down this huge crevasse. But Mr Dawson was wonderful. Called for help. Organized a rescue party. Got us to tie clothing together to make a rope. Went down there himself to rescue Jenks. Amazing. Real bravery. I couldn't have done it. No way.'

'Is this true?' asked Lanchester, leaning over the prone Potato-Head.

Dawson didn't have a choice. He could agree, or he could stack shelves in the Co-op. 'Er . . . yes . . . pretty much.'

'Hmmm . . .' Lanchester didn't have a choice either. He knew there was something fishy going on. He trusted Potato-Head only fractionally more than he trusted us. But masters stuck together. Team spirit, man. As he himself had said.

'Well,' said Grenade-Head, drawing in a deep, relieved lungful of antiseptic hospital air. 'I congratulate you on your swift actions, Mr Dawson. It seems as though you have averted a genuine catastrophe.'

'Thank you,' whispered Potato-Head to Barney as the two grown-ups disappeared through the curtain. 'That was very . . . very thoughtful of you.'

'Don't mention it,' said Barney. 'Just ease up on the homework for a term or two, yeh?'

The atmosphere was a touch strained on the journey back to the Centre. Potato-Head was lying flat-out on the floor in the back, urging Mr Lanchester to take the corners as slowly as possible. Unfortunately, however, Jenks was still totally out of his tree on the painkillers and was rolling around singing *Rudolph the Red-Nosed Reindeer* at the top of his voice.

Lanchester boiled with suppressed fury for the whole seventeen miles. Why was that vile child singing that damned song? Had confidential details of his private life been leaked? There was no way he could find out, in the present company. But if confidential details had been leaked, he knew who'd leaked them. And he threw the Land Rover as hard as he could into every hairpin bend to show that he knew.

It was 5 a.m. when we reached Plas Y Cyfoglyn. Lanchester had Potato-Head laid out on a table in the dining room so he could grill him in private about *Rudolph the Red-Nosed Reindeer*. The rest of us went upstairs to shower, apply Savlon and find spare trousers.

Jenks slept like a log, but Barney and I were still hyper. We packed our gear then headed downstairs. We were passing through the entrance hall when Grenade-Head sprinted into the office. We poked our heads around the door to hear a radio-receiver futting and crackling into life.

'Hey, Fforbesy. Check this out,' said the loudspeaker.

'What's a mobile phone doing up here?' replied the loudspeaker to itself.

It was Captain Prat and Fforbes-Giraffe. They must have woken up, wondered where the hell everyone had gone to, seen the flares and headed up through the wood. Evidently, Potato-Head hadn't discus-hurled his walkie-talkie far enough into the undergrowth.

'Reckon it works?' said Captain Prat.

'This is alpha-bravo,' chuckled Fforbes-Giraffe to himself, 'alpha-bravo calling all units. We're looking for some fat, middle-aged berk with a bandaged ear, over . . .'

'Easy, Justin. You don't know who's on the other end of that thing.'

Grenade-Head picked up the microphone, then paused, wanting to know the worst.

'What? That gorilla Michaels, you mean?' replied Captain Prat. 'I doubt he knows how to work a wrist-watch, let alone a mobile-phone.'

'God, where *do* they get the staff for these places?' sighed Fforbes-Giraffe.

'Borstals, probably.'

Etc. Etc.

Grenade-Head gave them enough rope to hang themselves good and proper, then pressed the SEND button on the microphone and slipped into Cyril-mode. 'Good morning, boys,' he hissed. 'I'm glad to hear that you're up and out of bed so early. May I suggest that you return to the Centre immediately? The toilets and the washrooms need scrubbing down, and you have just volunteered to do them all before you leave. Moreover, if I find one speck of dirt left when you have finished, I shall kick your backsides so hard you won't remember what day of the week it is. Is that perfectly clear? Good. I shall be seeing you shortly, then.'

Mel Carver led the Red team back at 8 a.m. to claim a plastic and brass trophy, even smaller and tackier than the trophy I won for the plasticine modelling prize at Infants.

Lesley appeared next, in a blue funk on account of having lost Babs. But there was nothing to fear. By some extraordinary coincidence, she had bumped into Dai Sideburn while wandering along a deserted mountain road in the small hours. He let her camp out in his flat above the Chinese down in the village and delivered her safely to the Centre ten minutes after Lesley.

Eleanor hadn't been quite so lucky. She woke up in pitch darkness at half-five to find that she had been abandoned by everyone except Penny Threadgold. Penny then woke up and proceeded to have some kind of panic attack on account of being so far away from streetlights and curling tongs and all the other necessary comforts of civilization. Still, as Eleanor said, after three hours of coping with Penny, she was, for the first time in her life, actually looking forward to spending time with a grandmother who mistook her for a dead cat.

Captain Prat and Fforbes-Giraffe never did come back. Grenade-Head was still standing by the jetty waiting for them to arrive when Mr Lanchester put the minibus into gear and pulled out of the drive.

I don't remember much of the journey. Potato-Head lay in the aisle reading articles about cellulite and body-hair in the crumpled *Cosmo* he had discovered lying under the back seat. Barney filled Jenks in on what had happened whilst his mind was out to lunch. Winston took out his keyboard and played bits of Mozart over the pre-set disco backing rhythm until his batteries died. And I began reading the opening chapters of the *Zombie Asteroid* trilogy which Roz had given me as a going-away present.

Elmo Dix, space joy-rider and galactic renegade, had just hot-wired a Zig 45 planet-hopper and blown his way out of the titanium airlock at the entrance to the multi-storey vehicle-park on the Ariston B space-station. But this wasn't to be his lucky day. He was only halfway back to Terra before the fuel gauges sagged dangerously into the red zone. There was an energy leak. He must have torn the fuselage on the airlock doors.

He swung into a holding orbit round a small asteroid and began scanning the StarCom frequencies for a passing trader-vessel. They might be persuaded to give him a tow. In fact, if they were looking down the wrong end of his laser-bazooka, they could probably be persuaded to swap ships.

And it was only then that he realized how very, very unlucky this particular day was going to turn out to be.

There was a flash of static on the vid-screen and he found himself staring at the ugly mug of Gröplön Doooo, the Neptunian villain he hadn't seen since their bloody shoot-out in the high-security moon-prison five years back. He was going to need more than a laser-bazooka to get himself out of this one.

'Elmo Dix. What a pleasant surprise,' gurgled Gröplön, his four ear-tongues flicking the midges away from his warty face. 'Welcome to my asteroid. I wonder . . . Perhaps you have brought me a new leg to replace the one you so cruelly removed from me during our last meeting . . .'

I was really getting into the story when Gröplön unexpectedly pulled a small, brown teddy bear from his vacuum compartment and said, 'He's called Diggles. The wife insisted I bring him along for the ride. Bit of an obsession with her, teddies. That and shelves. Can't move round this damned capsule for shelves . . .'

I was asleep.

The next thing I remember was Mum's head materializing round an opened minibus door. And behind her, on the illuminated grass outside the school entrance, a huge, multicoloured Z of flowering pansies.

'Oh look,' cooed Mum. 'The poor thing's completely wiped. They must have run him into the ground. Come on, Ben, wakey-wakey.'

I was home.

Battlestar III

Now that Irene had been imprisoned for possession of a naily plank with intent to commit GBH, Shirley assumed that she and Bruce Doggett would live together happily ever after. She was wrong. One Friday evening, when the coffee bar closed early because of a salmonella scare, she came home and found him prancing round the living room wearing the yellow taffeta ballgown she had bought to wear to the Lager Brewer's Association Annual Ball last summer. Something was not quite right. Bruce needed help. And fast.

'Bit kinky for this time in the evening . . .' I said, leaning over and helping myself to an Irish Cream.

'They've been trying to spice it up a bit over the past few weeks,' explained Mum. 'The ratings went through the floor when Channel 4 decided to put their Sumo wrestling programme on at the same time.'

'Makes sense,' I replied, heading for the kitchen. 'Just going to see what Dad's up to in the shed. Check he's not trying on your nightie, or anything.'

'Tea in five minutes,' she shouted as I disappeared into the garden.

'Howdy, pardner,' said Dad, as I closed the shed door behind me.

'Well, you can knock me down, step in my face, slander my name all over the place,' sang Elvis, from the battery cassette player.

'How's tricks?' I asked.

'. . . You can do anything that you want to do, but uh-uh honey, lay off of my shoes . . .'

'Tricks is groovy,' said Dad, holding some oily engine-gadgetoid up to the light.

Hoiking myself up on to the workbench I noticed my old catapult lying amongst the wrenches and spanners. 'How do you mend a car with this?'

'Oh that,' he smiled. 'You don't. Look. Come round here.' He picked up the catapult, went round to the far side of the bench, leant across it, picked up a spare nut and fitted it into the sling. 'Battlestar III,' he said, taking aim.

I looked across the shed. On the far side, sitting on top of the old lawnmower box, was the china sculpture of the street urchin balloon seller Gwen and Roger had given Mum and Dad the day they left Blakeney.

'Ptoing!' went the catapult.

'Tock!' went the nut on the wall.

'Zero points,' said Dad. 'Fancy a go? Two days and I haven't scored yet.'

I picked up a broken screw, loaded the catapult, tensed the rubber and let rip. The screw whacked the urchin in the head. A direct hit. But no points. The figurine rocked from side to side, then settled down again. That was all. Not a scratch.

'They must be making them in cast-iron these days,' said Dad, shaking his head, standing up and returning to his oily gadgetoid.

'The cod-pie's out of the oven,' said Mum, opening the shed door.

Dad cut Elvis off in mid-yodel.

'Yum City,' I said, putting the catapult down.

'What on earth is that for?' Mum asked, her eyes following the attack-trajectory from my hand, across the shed to the indestructible gwennie. 'Men,' she sighed. 'They just don't grow up, do they.'

As she was turning away there was a small, but audible 'Ker-lick!' from the top of the lawnmower box.

'What was that?' she asked, looking round.

Dad and I glanced up in time to see the cluster of brightly painted china balloons detach themselves from the wire string in the urchin's hand, topple sideways and shatter on the concrete floor.

We turned to each other, yelled 'Psychokinesis!' simultaneously and burst out laughing.

'Come on, children,' said Mum, wearily. 'Indoors.'

Still giggling, Dad put his arm round my shoulders and we headed up the path to sink the cod-pie.